Lock Down Publications and Ca$h
Presents

I0679208

BLOOD AND GAMES 2

Game Recognize Game

Written By
KING DREAM

First Edition 2024

Printed in the United States of America

Lock Down Publications
P.O. Box 944
Stockbridge, GA 30281
www.lockdownpublications.com

Like our page on Facebook: Lock Down Publications
www.facebook.com/lockdownpublications.ldp

Stay Connected with Us!

Text **LOCKDOWN** to 22828 to stay up-to-date with new releases, sneak peaks, contests and more…

Like our page on Facebook:
Lock Down Publications

Join Lock Down Publications/The New Era Reading Group

Visit our website:
www.lockdownpublications.com

Follow us on Instagram:
Lock Down Publications

Email Us: We want to hear from you!

Acknowledgements

Special thanks to Ca$h & the whole LDP family, Gary "G-Dub" Anderson, Patricia Vick & Krystal Williams for making the book possible.

Chapter 1

Fleetwood walked into the living room where Rome sat watching an old episode of Martin. "Well, pimp, it seems as though the pimp gods heard your prayers and are raining down their blessings upon you."

"What you talking about?"

Fleetwood picked up the remote.

"Don't change that channel."

"Trust me. You definitely want to see this." He turned to the news.

An Asian reporter woman stood in front of several burned down vehicles. The scene was taped off. Several police, firefighters, and EMS workers wandered around behind her. "I'm reporting live from south Holt Street where a car bomb detonated and set off a chain of car explosions. A man police have identified as Boss Bandz was reported as the only causality. What was supposed to be a quiet neighborhood now looks like a scene out of an action film. The police are casing the scene and speaking to witnesses. But so far no one has an idea of who planted the bomb that killed Boss Bandz and caused this devastating disaster you see before me. The family of Boss Bandz are stricken with grief and chose not to make any comments at the time. It's all been an unfortunate tragedy. I'm Patricia Wang reporting for Fox-6 News. Back to you, Stacy."

Fleetwood turned the TV down and took a seat on the couch. "That's some good news, huh?"

Rome had a look of confusion on his face. He couldn't believe what he was hearing. "Boss pushing up daisies? That's some damn good news." Rome rubbed his chin and a smile grew on his face. "Now you can get yo hoes back and jump back into the number two spot. And I don't have to worry about that young punk exposing me and coming for the throne. I must admit he did come real close."

"Yeah. But that chump got what he deserved. That was a sucka move, planting that dope on me just to get me out the way so he can get to my hoes." Rome had convinced Fleetwood that Boss was the one who set him up. And that Boss was a huge problem that they had to get rid of. Fleetwood was dying to get back at Boss for setting him up. Little did he knew he was only playing devil's advocate to the one who really set him up.

"I agree, that was some low-down dirty shit. On the bright side though, a message was renewed to any player in the game that thinks he can come for my crown. With life and death on the line they'll think twice before coming as close as Boss did."

"Dig that. So, what do we do now?"

"We go collect all his hoes and we prepare for the Player's Ball, baby." Rome sparked up a Newport cigarette. He took a hard pull causing the cherry tip to glow bright red. He sat back in his chair and blew out the cloud of smoke. Boss was gone and all his worries were now behind him.

***

Macita and the other girls sat around the kitchen table at Boss's house. The tears they had been shedding could've formed rivers. The pain of losing him took its toll on them all. With Queenie in the hospital still fighting for her life Isis felt it was time for her to take charge. "I need you all to listen up." All eyes turned to the end of the table where she sat, where Queenie used to sit. "Boss is gone. Queenie's barely hanging on and we got to move on." Before she could say another word Coco snapped at her.

"How dare you tell us when to move on! Bitch, you a newborn to this stable. What the fuck we look like taking orders from you?" Coco's words were felt all around the table.

"Newborn? I may be new to this family but I'm far from being new to the game. I've been in this game longer than most of you at this table." Isis slammed her hand on the table.

Macita chimed in. "I'm with Coco. I'm not going to listen to no bitch that's fresh to this family. For all I know you had something to do with Boss's murder and Queenie being in the hospital."

Isis jumped to her feet. "Bitch, if you saying I sold Boss out then come right out and say it!"

"Are you deaf or just a dumb, bitch? Because that's exactly what I just said!" Macita stood up to face Isis.

Coco stepped in between them to keep them from fighting. A big argument broke out between everyone at the table. Princess sat trying to calm Lil Boss. She rocked him as tears rolled down her face. Boss hadn't been gone two days and the family was already in shambles.

The arguing got louder and was two seconds to turning into another all-out war. "You bitches shut the fuck up and sit the fuck down! Now!" A woman yelled.

"You shut the fuck up!" Sandy, a 5'10" brunette that Boss had took from Fleetwood, caught up in the heat of the argument, responded without knowing who she was talking to. Everyone went quiet because they saw who she had misspoken to. Sandy turned around to see who they were looking at. An opened hand came flying her way and slapped across her face. "Ow!" She screamed and felt the side of her face.

"Watch your mouth when you talk to me."

"I apologize. I didn't know it was you Ms. Tweety."

Tweety looked around the room at all the startled faces. "My baby haven't been dead two days and y'all already pissing and shitting on everything he lived and died for. He gave his all to this family here he created. And y'all doing all you can right now to destroy it." The women felt ashamed of themselves.

"Ms. Tweety, what are you doing here?" Princess asked as she pulled out Boss's seat at the head of the table for her.

Tweety sat down and took out an ounce of weed and some blunts from her purse. She handed it to Stormy, the sexy Armenian chick Boss took from 6-9, who sat next to her. "Roll that up." Then she gestured for Princess to take a seat at the table. Princess took her seat and Tweety began to deliver the message she had for them. "Before Boss died, we had a discussion. I told him he should talk to a friend of the family that's with law enforcement. After what happened at the wedding, I wanted him to get protection against Rome. He looked me in the eyes and he said mama…" She paused to steady her voice and wipe the tears from her eyes before continuing. "He said, 'Mama, I know this shit is getting heavy but I rather die with the respect of a pimp than to live because I snitched. I'm going to be alright. But in case god has other plans for me I need you to do me a favor.'"

Stormy sparks a blunt and passes it to Tweety. All the women listen closely as she spoke.

"He said, 'Mama, take care of my family. All of them, and don't let Rome win. Finish my mission for me and take back the throne.'" She passed the blunt to Gemini who sat on the other side of her. Another blunt makes rotation Tweety's way.

"So, what are you saying, Ms. Tweety?" Gemini asked.

"What I'm saying is my baby is finna pimp from the grave. I'm taking over this family. And if anyone of you got a problem with that then speak now so I can set yo ass straight." Everyone remained quiet. "Good, now let's discuss the first measure of business." Tweety spent the better part of the evening discussing business with the girls then they reminisced about Boss.

Tweety didn't want to swim this far back in the game. She was comfortable with her current life and the steady tricks she had over the years. But for her son and late husband she would Michael Phelps her way through the ocean of the game to complete the mission they died for.

***

The same church they got married in now held Boss's funeral. The closed casket sat at the altar of the church. A poster sized picture of him was displayed next to his casket. Bouquets of flowers surrounded the altar. The church was packed with family, friends, and fellow pimps and whores. Boss's mother and his women along with Big Hunnid sat in the front row as the reverend delivered the eulogy.

"Let this show no man knows the hour God is gonna call him home." As the reverend went on the church doors opened up and in walks Rome and his whores along with Fleetwood Slim.

Murmurs erupted all through the church as he took a seat behind Tweety. Her blood boiled at the sight of him. She couldn't believe he was foul enough to show up at Boss's funeral and have the audacity to sit right behind her.

As Reverend began to close with a prayer, Rome leaned in and whispered to Tweety. "Tweety, I am terribly sorry for your loss. If there's anything I can do for you, please let me know."

It took everything in her not to pull her Glock 40 out her purse and push his top back. Instead, she kept her cool. "I see you've been toasting well to my sorrows. I can still smell the celebration of my son's death on your breath. You have some nerve showing up here. Understand something, I've never needed and won't ever need anything from you, ever.

Now if you got something more to say then you wait until I'm finished paying my respects to what was my only child."

Rome eased back in his seat with a smile.

Everyone filed out the church doors behind the pallbearers. Tweety watched as they loaded Boss's casket into the hearse.

"I'm sorry for your loss, mama." A voice came from behind her.

She turned towards the familiar voice then wrapped her arms around him. "Polo, baby I'm so glad you came."

"Me, too."

"Boss is smiling down to see you here. You know even though y'all had y'all little issue, he never stopped loving you like a brother."

"I know, mama. And I hate I let things get in the way of our bond. It kills me that it's too late for me to even apologize and make things right between him and me." Polo's voice broke off into a sob.

Tweety hugged him. "It's okay, baby. I'm sure Boss knew you didn't really feel that wat." As Tweety embraced Polo, Princess walked up behind him.

"Mama, could you hold Lil Boss for a second?"

At the sound of Princess's voice Polo turned around. He couldn't believe what he was seeing. Princess was even more gorgeous than she was when he first met her. He seen her a few times without her noticing after she got out the hospital. And he was proud at how messed up she looked because he knew nobody would want her. But now she no longer had the rough scars and awkward shaped nose he left her with. She was drop-dead gorgeous. Her red skin glowed like a ray of sunshine. She still had the body of Kim Kardashian. It's of no doubt Boss spent some cheese to get her back right. "Princess?"

Princess was shocked to see who turned around. "Polo? What are you doing here?"

Tweety, seeing they had something's to talk about, excused herself. "Give me Lil Boss and y'all go 'head and talk. And Polo, keep yo hands to yo self, you hear me?"

"Yes, ma'am."

She walks off with Lil Boss in her arms.

"Lil Boss? You and Boss had a baby?"

"Yes, he's Boss's son."

"So, I was right. Y'all was messing around behind my back."

"That's what you want to talk to me about? After all this time instead of an apology for all you put me through, you want to discuss whether or not me and Boss was creeping? And out of all places, his funeral! You know what? I'll oblige your question. No, Boss and I were not messing around while you and I were together. Boss was too loyal of a friend to you."

"Loyal? How so when the two of you still ended up together, and had a baby?"

"You pushed us together," Princess said pointing at him. "Boss didn't want to get with me. You know why he originally took me in? I tell you what he told me when I first approached him about him and I being together. He said he took me in because he knew how much I meant to you. And that when you got life together, I would be right there waiting on you. So, yeah, Boss was real loyal to you. I'm the one who convinced him that there was no more you and I and that it was him that I always wanted, not you."

They say the truth hurts and Polo felt every pain of it. "Well, Boss is not here anymore. So, it's time you start thinking about coming back home." Polo buttoned the button on his suit jacket.

"Come back home? Wow, you are truly unbelievable. They haven't even put my son's father in the grave yet and you already trying to get at me?"

"Yeah, well you were mines first. I found you."

Princess turned around at the sound of her name being called.

"Princess, we got to go, sweety!" Tweety yelled over to Princess from the limo.

She turned back to Polo. "Well finders keepers, loser weepers. Dead or alive I will always belong to Boss." She walked off to the limo.

Some pimps may have thought Boss was on some square shit with Princess by caring for her like he did. But in actuality he was displaying his mastery in the art of selling love. He learned from the Holy Bible of Game that a hoe like Princess is worth investing in. Princess seen him as a god before she lost her good looks. So, with him taking her in at her worst, showing her a pimp's love and building her back up, he was creating a thoroughbred that would help shake the game up and bring him to new levels. And that game worked so well that even now that he's dead she still remained loyal to his name.

Chapter 2

Isis sits in her hotel room awaiting a new client she caught off the internet. Her heart was still in shambles and didn't really feel like working. But like Tweety told her, "Life goes on with you or without you, so live it while you can." She could almost hear Boss's voice saying, "Bitch, I don't care if it wasn't a single breath left in my lungs. You better get my mothafuck'n money!" That thought alone brought a smile to her face. But the thought of him being gone made her want to break down.

A knock on her room door put a halt to her tears before they could begin to run. "Just a minute!" She yelled to the door as she dabbed the corners of her eyes with a handkerchief. She opened the door and her soul could've flew from her body.

"You look surprised to see me, baby. I see you still posting on nudeafrica.com to catch your tricks." He pushed passed her and walked in.

"What are you doing here, Rome?"

"I'm here to offer you my forgiveness. So, pack your stuff up and let's go home."

Isis stayed close to the open door in case she had to make a break for it. "I don't need your forgiveness and I have a home."

Rome spun around and came towards her. She couldn't get her feet to move. It felt like she was standing in quicksand. He walked up on her. "Bitch, you coming home with me. You ain't got no daddy no more, so hoe, what home do you have?"

"Her home is here with me. That's my bitch now," Tweety said from the doorway.

Both Rome and Isis looked her way. "If it isn't Angela Tweety Bird Marjonnie."

"It's Bandz, not Marjonnie."

"Whatever. You still looking good, baby."

Tweety makes a head gesture at Isis. "Isis, go join the other girls downstairs."

"But, Ms. Tweety—"

Tweety puts up her hand, silencing her. "Bitch, do as I said and not a word more!"

Isis didn't want to leave Tweety alone in the room with that monster but did as she was told.

Tweety takes post against the long dresser with her jacket folded over her arm.

Rome cracked up laughing. "You? You trading your stilettos in for some gators? Come on now. You a hoe, not a pimp. You couldn't be doing nothing more than running a rest haven for these hoes." He continued laughing.

"Did you forget the true king of this game was my husband? And if you think about it, he pimped you, too."

Rome's grinned was now replaced with a mug. "Look here, bitch, that worm food ass nigga Cadillac never pimped me!"

Tweety smiled seeing she struck his nerve. "Well, if that's what you choose to believe. I just never met a pimp who hoes paid him and he paid another pimp."

Feeling Tweety had crushed his last nerve he wanted to crush her windpipe. He tried to snatch her up, but she was already steps ahead of him. Before he could come any closer, he seen she had her Glock 40 pointed at him from under the jacket that was wrapped around her arm.

"Cadillac taught me how to be ten steps ahead of niggas like you. And if you move any closer, I'm going to show you what he taught me next. I know you had something to do with the deaths of my husband and my son. So please give me a reason to pull this trigger."

"If you think that then why don't you pull that trigger?"

"Because death is too easy for you. I'm going to give it to you where it hurts. I'm going to take the crown right off your head."

Rome's smile returned. "You think you got what it takes for this game?"

"Honey, I don't just think, I know. I was a bottom bitch, so running hoes is what I do best."

"You see, many have come for the crown and many have died trying to get it. Understand Tweety, this is a dangerous game."

"Good, because there's no fun in playing it safe."

"Then game on." He walked out the room.

***

"Sellout ass bitch!" Peaches yelled to Isis in the hotel parking lot.

"Who the fuck you calling a sellout?"

"You, you disloyal ass bitch."

"What? You mad because I upgraded? You should be thanking me for giving you the room to be Rome's bottom bitch. But I guess your poor hustling ass still couldn't compete with Ashley and Hannah here." Isis nodded her head towards Rome's two white whores.

"Don't listen to her, Peaches. She's just mad because she's washed up. Rome already said he was about to get rid of her anyway," Hannah told Peaches. Hannah was a 24-year-old blonde with ocean blue eyes. Her perky 38DD breast were always the first thing you'd notice when you saw her. To everyone's surprise they were all natural. Like most white girls she had no ass and a Valley Girl personality. She took over as Rome's bottom bitch.

"He was about to dismiss me? Bitch, you so blonde and dumb it's funny. If he was going to get rid of me and I'm supposed to be so washed up, then why is he here trying to get me to come back home with him?"

"Because you're a charity case," Ashley says shrugging her shoulders. Ashley was a 5'11" long-legged, strawberry blonde with hazel green eyes. She had a 36C breast size and gorgeous legs. Ashley was 20 years old with an *I just want to fight* attitude.

"What? He pimping for the Salvation Army or something? Because real pimps don't do charity, hoe." Gemini buts in with.

"Why y'all all in our business? What y'all silly hoes need to be worried about is why y'all daddy supposed to be king pimp and only have three hoes." Coco added in.

"At least we got a daddy, you bastard ass hoes!" Peaches retorted.

Macita jumped in. "Oh, I know this bitch didn't go there."

Then all hell broke loose. It was an all-out brawl. Isis, Gemini, Coco and Macita tore into Peaches, Ashley and Hannah's asses. Hair tracks and blonde extensions littered the parking lot as the girls went at it.

"I never liked yo punk ass anyway, bitch." Gemini slammed her fist into Ashley's face.

"Get the fuck off her!" Rome came pulling Gemini off Hannah and throwing her against the door of a truck setting, its alarm off. All the girls stopped fighting. "Get y'all ass in the fucking car." Peaches, Ashley and Hannah did as they were told, mugging the other girls as they got in Rome's Mercedes truck. He stared over at Tweety's girls. "I should break my foot off in you hoes' asses for fucking up my bitch's face."

"Don't blame us! Blame their parent's because them hoes' faces was fucked up way before we got ahold of them." Gemini shot back at him.

Her retort pissed Rome off. "What you say, bitch?"

"I said—"

SMACK! Rome slapped the words right out her mouth, busting her lip in the process.

Gemini touched her finger to her lip and seen the blood on the tip of her finger. "Hell nah! Don't no nigga put his hands on me." She went for the gun under the passenger seat of Tweety's Escalade.

Tweety showed up in time to stop her before her shaking hands could raise the gun. "Give it to me. I got this."

With her face red with anger, embarrassment and from the slap Rome gave her she reluctantly handed the gun over to Tweety.

She slipped it back under the seat before turning to Rome. "You keep your hands off my girls, Rome. Or you and I are going to have some problems that can't be solved with words."

"I ain't worried about you. You tell them hood rats to respect a pimp and to keep their hands off my women. If they can do that then they won't have to worry about my foot in their ass." Rome got in his truck and pulled off.

Tweety looked up to the sky. "You Bandz men better give me the strength not to kill that man before I finish this mission." Everybody loaded up in her Escalade. Looking in her review mirror she could see Gemini was still shaken up and on the edge of hyperventilating. She knew why too. She passed her a paper bag. "Breathe in that bag, baby, until your nerves calm."

The paper bag inflated and deflated as she breathed in and out of it.

Boss told Tweety about what happened to her when she was a little girl. Gemini was a 5'1" feisty little Asian and white mixed chick, small perky breast and little ass. But the tricks loved her boyish shaped body. She grew up in upper middle class. Her mom and dad were both archeologists. One day they were on a dig inside an ancient mine in Africa and something went wrong and the mine caved in on them.

A large boulder fell on top of them, crushing and killing them instantly. With no other relatives or anyone to take her in she was juggled around in the foster care system. The foster homes she lived in were some of the worst. She was constantly beat on by the other kids and the foster parents seen her as nothing more than a check. When she finally did get adopted by a middle-aged white couple that lived in the suburbs, she thought her troubles were over. But she couldn't have been more wrong.

The mother of the house, Sally, was a nurse who worked long and undetermined hours. At times she would get paged to come in late at night or while they were in the middle of having family time. The father, Rick, was a real estate developer. Everything seemed fine the first few months after the adoption. Then one night Sally was paged in and Rick crept into Gemini's room. She would try to tell Sally about it, but Sally refused to believe her. And her reward for telling was Sally would beat her then Rick would beat her when Sally left for telling. She knew Sally honestly believed her, but Sally felt that it was her fault Rick was a sick ass baby-raper because she had to work such long hours. After a while Rick didn't even have to hide what he was doing to Gemini from Sally. She accepted it. This abuse had become a routine thing. She would cry herself to sleep every night wondering why God hated her so much that he would take her parents away from her and make her suffer through so much.

One day when she was 16, she had had enough of their abuse. She told them she had stopped taking her birth control and showed them a pregnancy test. She told them if they didn't sign the papers for her to be emancipated, she would go to the police and tell them to do the DNA test so they could see Rick's the father. Neither one of them wanting to go down for rape and abuse charges and smear their good Christian names, agreed to sign the papers. Once everything went through, they gave her money for an abortion and to keep quiet, and sent her on her way. Little did they know she was never pregnant. She was running the game on them that Break-A-Hoe had told her to run. And it worked like a charm.

"You feel better?"

"Yes." Gemini passed the bag back to her.

"Ms. Tweety, how did you know when to come up there when you did? I didn't even have the opportunity to send out any distress signal to you." Isis asked.

"It's my job to know when my girls are in trouble and to come to their rescue when they need me. I know this game like Michael Jordan knows basketball. I know how a pimp thinks and how a hoe thinks. It's not much that can get past me. I knew it wouldn't be long before Rome showed up to try and get you and the rest of the girls. And I damn sure wasn't going to let that man take anyone else from me." The silence filled the truck as they all thought about all the losses Tweety had taken because of Rome.

Then Coco switched the conversation to Gemini. "Yo, your wild ass nailed that bitch Hannah good! That hoe's head was bouncing off your fist like you had trampoline knuckles."

Everybody bust out laughing. Then they started talking about how they beat up the other girls.

While they were busy laughing and giggling, Tweety was plotting her next move against Rome. To make her next move work she needed leverage. Her phone buzzed with a text message. And the text that just came through on her phone told her just how to get the leverage she needed.

Chapter 3

Isis walked into the kitchen and grabbed a bottled water out the refrigerator. She heard Lil Boss giggle and splashing in the water as Princess gave him a bath in the sink. "He's getting big isn't he?"

"As much as he eats, he better be. In a minute we going to have to recruit some more hoes or this boy is gonna eat us out a house and home."

They both laughed.

Isis stood next to Princess. She smiled down at Lil Boss and tickled his stomach. He smiled back at her and let out a high pitched laugh. "How you been holding up?"

"I should be asking you that question." Isis responded.

"Well, for me it's been a challenge not having Boss here. It hurts to know that he won't be here to see Lil Boss take his first steps, say his first words and everything else. But I know I got to be strong for our little man. Just like Tweety was strong for Boss when his father died. With all the support I have from you, Tweety and the rest of the family I know we'll be okay. And you?"

Isis releases a deep breath from her lungs. "I can't lie, I feel angry, cheated. It's like I spent so much time trying to fuck him over to please another man and when my heart finally fell into Boss's hands our love was short-lived."

"I know exactly how you feel. I could tell from the first time I met you at the club you really had a thing for him.

Remember when Boss sent Queenie and all of us over there to run the reverse Charlie on you?"

"Yes!" Isis shot a playful scowl at Princess.

"Your ass was so heated you was turning redder than a tomato." Princess laughed at the memory.

"I was pissed."

"Yes, you were. But I could tell it really was more to it than being pissed that he beat you at your own game. You were starting to catch feelings for him. And when he brought you home, I could see you felt that missing puzzle piece to your heart was finally found."

"And how did you know all that?"

"Because he gave me those same feelings. So, I know your feelings for him were genuine."

"Well at least you could see that. You know most of the other girls still think I had something to do with what happened to him and Queenie."

"Of course, they do. And you can't blame them. They're hurt and don't know who to blame for their pain. And you was his enemy's bottom bitch and you and Queenie was at odds. So, it's only natural they place their suspicion on you. But trust me, they're slowly reevaluating their thoughts on you."

"Why you think that?"

"Because you still here representing team Bandz. Even though Boss is gone, you still didn't go running back to Rome. That says a lot about you. And if they can't see your loyalty and love for him through that then I'll help you beat some sense into them bitches. Ain't that right, baby? Mama will kick they ass." She rubs her nose against Lil Boss's cheek, making him giggle.

"I see Polo showed up to the funeral."

"He came and talked to me at the end." Princess's playful mood turned dull.

"Did you—"

"NO!" Princess cut her off, already knowing what Isis wanted to know.

"Understood." Isis put her hands up as if she was surrendering.

"Sorry." Princess stood Lil Boss up and dried him off. "I mean, could you believe this mothafucka had the nerve to try to get with me at the funeral? And, like, no apology for what he did to me or shit? He thinks because Boss is gone I'm going to come back to him. I don't think so. I think he's up to something though."

"Like what?"

"I don't know. But did you see his eyes?"

"What about them?"

"They ain't the same. He ain't the same."

"What do you mean?"

"Polo was a fun and hilarious person to be around and you could've seen that in his eyes. But now, if you look into them, it's like there's nothing. Just darkness. Not a sign of life in him as if he no longer has a soul." She stared off into a daze.

"Oh my god! Princess, he spraying everywhere! Cover that thing up!" Isis screamed as Lil Boss peed all over them.

"Lil Boss!" They both yelled in unison and cracked up laughing.

While Princess and Isis were busy getting pissed on, Polo was busy being pissed off. "This bitch had this nigga's baby, then think I'm dumb enough to believe they weren't seeing each other behind my back." Polo drank a beer and shot darts at Boss's obituary.

"Baby, stop mourning over the love you shared with that bitch. You got me now. And I'm all the woman you'll ever need." She wrapped her arms around his neck and planted a soft kiss on his lips.

"You don't get it do you, Peaches?" Polo yanked her arms off him. "This is no longer about love. This is about avenging my respect. That bitch and Boss played me for stupid. Completely taking my loyalty for granted and insulted my intelligence in the process. Neither one of them ever thought I truly had what it takes to succeed in this game. So, I'm going to show them, well her, by taking the crown myself." He took a swig of his beer. "And you going to help me do it." He shot two more darts in quick procession, this time at a picture he printed off Princess's Snapchat page. A picture of her pushing Lil Boss in a swing at the park. The first dart lands directly in the mouth of a smiling Princess and the second one finds its home in the center of Lil Boss's forehead.

"What do you want me to do?"

"You going to get me in good with Rome so he can teach me everything he knows about the game."

"Baby, you know Rome don't even rock that close with Fleetwood and that's his right hand."

"Don't worry about that. You just get me in the door. I'm hungry enough to find my way to the kitchen."

Peaches took the beer out his hand and drank from it. "Consider it done...daddy."

Polo and Peaches kept a low-key relationship since the night Boss got Charlied. Everything between them went on pause when he met Princess. It boiled Peaches's blood when he cut her off, but she knew it would be only a matter of time before he would be back. She could see Princess was out of his league. Princess possessed a love for the game and the ambition to make her man number one. Polo, on the other hand, wanted his cake and eat it too. He liked the idea of being called a pimp but expected a square type relationship with his hoe. Peaches seen that the first week they started kicking it. She agreed to stop hoeing and pursue modeling and a career as a video vixen. He understood she couldn't just up and leave Rome without a solid foundation to run to. And to build a solid foundation, they had to get their money up.

Lately she's been cuffing money and sliding it to Polo to stack for them. They figured 20G's would be a good enough head start for them. But now Polo wanted to put those plans on hold and take over the pimp game. Little did Peaches know he planned to become king and make Princess his queen, and not her. Seeing Princess again at the funeral reminded him of what his heart's been missing. And if Princess wasn't going to go, he was going to make her life a living hell until she came to her senses and chose to be with him.

Chapter 4

Tweety brought the Wraith to a stop in front of a white duplex apartment on 18th and Meineckee Street. It was an area of Milwaukee the city labeled Ghost Town. Twins Lulu and Skittles sat on the porch. A man sat between Lulu's legs while she twisted his dreads and greased his scalp. Skittles was drinking red Kool-Aid out of a pickle jar and pouring a bottle of Louisiana Hot sauce inside a big bag of Flaming Hot Cheetos. They chanted "Aye, aye, get that shit," as a group of girls in front of their house twerked to the song *Body* by Megan Thee Stallion. When they see the Rolls Royce pull up they all stopped dancing and admired the car.

Tweety honked the horn. Lulu pushed the man between her legs forward and stood up. She skank-walked to the car with Skittles behind her sucking hot sauce and Flaming Hot Cheeto dust off her fingers.

Lulu and Skittles were hood rats, but they were also two of the coldest boosters in the Midwest. The bitches were so good at what they do they could steal the clothes off a runway model and be gone before she knew she was naked. Their mama Chrissy used to prostitute with Tweety back in the day until she got strung out on drugs. Tweety used to look out for the twins when Chrissy would go off on her drug binges and leave them for days in the house hungry and alone. The twins adopted her as their aunty and Tweety was happy to have them as her nieces. Thieves like them always came in handy.

Skittles hopped in the backseat and Lulu in the front. "Damn, aunty, you riding fly as a bitch!" The ice cubes clinked against the glass as Skittles took a sip of her Kool-Aid.

"Skittles, you spill that Kool-Aid or waste those chips in this car and I'm gonna bury my stilettoes in your ass. Matter-of-fact, get that shit out of here."

Skittles opened the door. "Meka, here! Hold this until I get out the car."

A dark-skinned girl with a ponytail that was so short it could barely fit in a rubber band walked over.

Skittles gave her the chips and Kool-Aid. "Don't eat and drink up all my stuff either!"

Meka waved her off and walked away.

"I see you got my text message."

"Lulu, you said something about having some evidence that could put a stake in that blood-sucking Rome's heart?"

"Yup."

"What you got?"

Lulu handed her a file and a memory stick.

Tweety flipped through the file. "How did you get this?"

"You know how we do, TT Tweety," Skittles said loud and proudly from the backseat.

"A homeboy I know was looking for some camera equipment to start a photography business. Me and Skittles happened to run into this private investigator who left his bag of equipment unattended in his car while he ran into the gas station."

"That fool thought setting his car alarm was going to stop bitches like us from getting what we want. We had all his shit in our car and gone in thirty seconds. It should've been a world record."

"We took all the equipment and stuff back to the crib to see what all we got. We were price-checking everything so we'd know what to charge my homeboy for it all when we came across all that. We figured it was exactly what you needed."

Tweety was still flipping through the file and a smile crept upon her face. "And y'all figured right." Tweety stuffed the file between her seat and the center console and put the memory stick in her purse. Then she took out some money and peeled off three hundred a piece for them and took off.

She made her way to the hospital to check on Queenie. An officer sat outside her room. After all that's been going on it was deemed necessary for her to have protection all around the clock. She signed in on the clipboard the officer held. She also checked the sign-in sheet to see who all had been to visit her. She seen Tina's, Marjorie's, and Princess's name on the list.

"Ms. Bandz! " The doctor harnessed her attention before she could walk into the room.

"Yes, doctor?"

"I thought I would give you the good news before you go in there."

"What news might that be?"

"Mrs. Bandz has awakened."

Tweety didn't stand by to wait for another word to be said. She rushed into the room. The movie *Coming to America* played on the television. Queenie's eyes were wide open staring at the screen. Tweety wasted no time wrapping her arms around her in a fit of excitement. "Thank God. I knew you'd pull through. How you feeling?"

Queenie didn't respond. She just stared up at Tweety.

"Can you hear me?"

"She can hear you just fine."

"Then why isn't she responding?"

"She doesn't know how to speak. The motor skills part of her brain was damaged, disabling her ability to properly use her vocals or walk. She can make noises, grunts, moans, cries and things like that. But she can't form words."

"Is it permanent?"

"It might or might not be. We don't quite know as of yet. These things are unpredictable. The brain is a complicated organ. We hope with therapy she will learn to speak and walk again."

Tweety took ahold of Queenie's hand. "Keep fighting, Queenie. You will walk and talk again. I know it." She looked down at what seemed to be an empty shell of the woman she once knew and groomed to be the perfect bottom bitch. But when she looked into the eyes that stared back at her she seen that woman she once knew still inside and fighting to find her way back to surface. Tweety was going to help her find her voice and legs again. No matter how long it may take, she wasn't going to give up on her. Because even though Boss was no longer with them, Tweety was determined to keep his vow of through sickness and health. She believed in family, loyalty and in her eyes, Queenie was no less family to her than any blood relative. So, it was no second thought to be had as to where her home was. She was a Bandz and would always be one.

Chapter 5

Tweety sat behind the wheel of Boss's Wraith. She was parked on the corner of 29th and Wisconsin Street watching Rome and Fleetwood converse with some other pimps outside of Lenny's Pool Hall. Coco jumps in and closes the door.

"Did you take care of that?"

"I did just like you told me to."

"Good. Then our friend will be contacting us shortly." Tweety rested her elbow on the armrest and flicked her fingernails while she stared at Rome and Fleetwood.

"Mane, I hear the late, great Cadillac Bandz old bottom bitch is pimping now," Pimping Icy Blue told the other pimps standing around outside of Lenny's.

"Then you better lock your whores up, Icy, because word is her tongue is longer than your dick," Pimping Ball said and they all cracked up laughing.

"On a serious note, she inherited all Boss's hoes. That's a mean team to be playing with, Jack. And she's determined to take over the throne in Boss's honor." Tony Swag added before Icy Blue spoke his mind.

"Granted she still fine enough to spin minds, take dimes, and maybe earn a little bit of my time. But you think some old whore could really step foot in a man's game and take over the throne?"

Big Hunnid stepped forward and began to speak up for his sister. "Look who her pimp was. Cadillac Bandz was the greatest pimp alive. When he was killed Boss was just a boy. And we all seen the extraordinary game Boss displayed, right?" All the men except Rome and Fleetwood agreed. "So, who y'all think taught him the game coming up? Tweety! And that should show you game-spitters that this bitch is a force to be reckoned with."

The players began to see his point. That was everyone but Rome and his sidekick.

"A force to be reckoned with? Cadillac Bandz is long-lived. I'm the king now and been the king for years and will continue to reign king until there's not a breath left in my lungs! Boss tried to come for the throne, but may he rest in peace. And Tweety ain't shit but a washed-up whore playing pimp. The only way she would come close to sitting on the throne is if she was riding my big, black dick while I sat on it." Rome then took a puff of his cigar and blew out the smoke.

"I hear you, Rome, but player to player, she's your ex hoe and my sister. We both know this bitch is something serious. And to underestimate her will be a serious mistake." Big Hunnid stared Rome dead in the eyes.

Rome slowly blew out a train of smoke then stepped closer to Big Hunnid. "I...ain't...worried," he said slowly to Big Hunnid but loud enough for all the others to hear. Rome searched Big Hunnid's eyes for an understanding then puts his cigar back in his mouth and walked off. Fleetwood accompanied him. "Can you believe the nerve of these niggas, Fleet? They worried about a bitch, a ex whore of mine taking over the game. Then think I should be worried. I tamed that bitch once before and I'll tame her ass again." They stop beside his Mercedes AMG.

"So what you had in mind?" Rome chirped the alarm.

"Get in and I'll tell just what we're going to do about that yellow bitch."

After Rome laid out the plan to get rid of Tweety, Fleetwood got out and walked to his car. He chirps the alarm on his white on white '87 Fleetwood Brougham that sat on trues and vogues. Before he got in, he picked up an envelope that sat in the driver's seat. Someone must've slipped it in through the driver's window he left cracked open. He kept his windows cracked to keep the heat from the sun from cracking the leather. He got in, tossing the envelope to the side for later viewing. Right then he had other things more beneficial to do. He just met a 20-year-old white girl named Amy and her 19-year-old cousin Jennifer a few days ago at the mall. They texted him while he was in the car with Rome, letting him know they were ready to get on his team. That was just the news he needed. Ever since Boss had knocked him for his stable he'd been itching to get some hoes on his team.

At 46 years old, 6'1", brown skin with a slender build and short fade with waves, Fleetwood wasn't a bad looking brother. He kept a cleanly shaved face with a neatly trimmed mustache and wore nothing but top of the line suits. It'd been a few black women who wanted to get on his team. But Fleetwood only wanted white women in his stable. He seen white women as being more profitable and less problematic. A black woman was too much headache for him.

He picked up Amy and Jennifer from the mall he first met them at. They rode around smoking and kicking it for a couple of hours while he kicked game and his expectations to them. They were more than excited to be with a real-life pimp. They'd only seen pimps in movies.

Fleetwood drove them out to Iowa and got them a room. After telling them how to take care of business he got inside his car and waited as they got ready to turn their first trick. He started the car up. The radio played *Make Me Say It Again* by the Isley brothers. Feeling good he sang along with the music. He reached down and activated the air-conditioning. It came on full blast and he turned it down. Then from the corner of his eye he seen something from the passenger side fall to the floor. He glanced over and seen the envelope from earlier. He had forgotten all about it. He picked up the envelope and opened it up. He couldn't believe his eyes. No way what he was seeing could be true. But then again, knowing who he was dealing with, anything was possible.

He took out his phone and called the number that was left for him.

They answered on the sixth ring. "I see you got my message," Tweety voiced on the other end.

"Anybody could falsify documents. I want more proof."

"Understandable. I can give you all the proof you need. But in return I got some things I want you to do for me."

"Sounds like a deal to me."

"Meet me at the casino at eleven o'clock, Friday night."

"I'll be there."

***

The shouts of winners' excitement and the cursing of losers made the perfect adlibs to the musical sound of the slot machines ringing as they played their game of pay-and-take with its gamblers. Fleetwood passed by a craps table. A set of dice slapped against the wall of the table landing a hard seven. The crowd around erupts into cheers. Fleetwood paid no mind as he scanned the casino for Tweety.

He locates her at Lucky Toads slot machines playing the slots. He walked over and took occupancy of the empty seat next to her.

"You late," Tweety told him without taking her eyes off her machine. She pressed buttons on the machine and puffed on a Black & Mild. She wore a silk, black Versace dress that hugged her every curve. Her long, wavy red hair she wore down looked as if it were a red waterfall flowing down her back.

Fleetwood looked at his watch. "It's only 11:13."

"That's 13 minutes of my time you just lost out on. So, forgive yourself when this conversation is cut short."

"I didn't come here to be lectured to by a bitch about punctuality."

"No, you came to get some evidence and information you so desperately need from this Bitch. So, if I were you I would mind my tongue and maybe kiss my ass a little."

"Kiss your ass? Let's not act like you doing this for charity. You already let it be known you want something out of this." He sparked up a cigarette.

"Fair. You got a copy of the file showing Rome's been cooperating with those two detectives that made the news. And you got the photos of him with the two of them." She passed him her cellphone with a voice recording ready to be queued up. "Now press play and you'll have all the evidence you need."

He pressed the play button on the screen. The sound of two car doors slamming are heard followed by the voices of Shaw and Perkins. "Damn Shaw, did you see the ass on officer Johnson in those pants?"

"Oh, yeah, it was like two hams perfectly stuffed back there. I'm a breast man myself but Lisa Johnson could definitely get it." The sound of a phone ringing is heard next. "It's our friend Rome."

"What do this jackass want now? Put him on speaker."

"Yeah, it's Shaw." He answered.

Rome's voice came blaring through the speakerphone. "Shaw, I need you and Perkins to take care of something for me."

"Aren't you about out of favors from us?"

"For the kind of money I pay the both you, I shouldn't be."

"What do you need, Rome?"

"I need Fleetwood out the way. Just for a little while."

"Fleetwood? Your main man Fleetwood? What the hell did he do? Take one of your whores from you or something?"

"I don't pay y'all to question me why."

"Fine, I could care less anyways. When you say a little while, how long are we talking?"

"No more than a year."

"Well, maybe we'll pull him over for an illegal lane change. And when we walk up to his car, we smell the heavy odor of marijuana coming from inside. Upon further inspection we find a half ounce of cocaine. That would buy him about six months or maybe a year at the most to sit down and think about what he did."

"Sounds like a plan. I'll call you back with the time and where you could find him after I plant the coke in his car."

"Cool. But what about our money?"

"I will feed you pigs when Fleetwood is behind bars! So, the faster you do your job, the faster you'll get your money!" Rome's phone disconnected the call.

"Can you believe this jackass?"

"That's a dirty son of a bitch to setup his own best friend. It makes you think who you can really trust these days."

Fleetwood ends the recording.

Tweety pulled the lever on the slot machine and looked over at him while blowing a cloud of smoke out. "You never bothered to ask yourself what was two Milwaukee detectives doing in Brown County pulling you over?

"No. That's exactly how everything played out, too. Those two dicks pulled me over, talking about I made a illegal lane change. Then searched the car because they said it smelled like weed. And that's when they found the dope under the dashboard. I can't believe this dirty mothafucka played me out like that!"

Tweety laughed.

"What the hell you find so funny about this?"

"What did you think would happen if you played with a snake? Eventually he was gonna bite your ass. Let me guess. He made you think it was Boss that set you up?"

"His words were Boss got me out the way to get to my bitches. How could I not believe it when I come home and Boss had knocked all three of my women?"

"Rome knew Boss would win against you in a challenge. And that would leave him open to be challenged by Boss. With you out the way, Boss couldn't challenge you. Which means he couldn't challenge Rome. But Rome didn't expect Boss to find a loophole in the game."

"Even I have to admit that was some slick shit to knock me for my bitches to secure the number two spot without challenging me."

"Indeed. When Boss did that, Rome had to do something to get him out the way. So, he lied to you about Boss setting you up so that you would go after Boss."

"I see. But Tweety, it wasn't me who killed Boss or shot Queenie. I had nothing to do with that."

Tweety stared at him a second then turned back to pressing buttons and pulling the lever on the slot machine. "I know you didn't, Fleet. You play with snakes and do some dirty shit, but you ain't no killer. I can't say the same thing about your friend Rome."

"I don't think he had anything to do with it either."

"And why is that?"

"Because he thinks I was the one who done it."

Tweety paused a moment. "Then who you think did it?"

Fleetwood shrugged his shoulders. "I have no clue. Though the word I heard on the low was that bitch Boss had that overdosed."

"Cherry?"

"Yeah. Word was that before she took that ride to the pearly white gates, she ordered a hit out on Queenie. So, I'm thinking maybe Boss got caught in the middle. I guess you got to blame an angel and not the devil for this one."

"Maybe, but I have a gut feeling that Rome has more to do with this than we both know. And my gut has never been wrong."

"So, what it is you want from me?"

"I know he's been plotting against me. And I know he's ran his plot by you. Tell me what he has planned and then I'll tell you what it is I need from you." She pulled the lever and the slot machine goes crazy when it's reels land on three flaming red toads.

"I guess it's your lucky night all the way around the board."

Chapter 6

Rome steadied his hand as he moved the pool stick back and forth between his fingers. Then with the precision of a marksman he hits his target, sending the cue ball speeding to the triangle of balls separating them with a loud blast. The yellow ball goes in the left side pocket as the red one goes into the left corner pocket and green one rolls back towards him, falling into the right corner pocket. "Solids it is, Jack," Rome told Tony Swag while chalking the tip of his stick.

They stood in Rome's basement that he had converted into his own little Boom Boom Room. The room was decorated with a full bar and bar stools, marble floors, two stripper poles, a sound system, some bar-style tables, a pool table and 100" flat screen TV. Several other pimps and whores sat around smoking, drinking, kicking the shit and snorting lines of powder as they played pool.

"More Breaking News about the two detectives authorities say were under investigation for the shooting death three weeks ago of an unarmed black man in the Hill Side area." The news reporter announced.

"Turn that up!" Rome ordered.

Fleetwood switches off the music and raises the TV volume on the sound system.

"Rumors say these two men, detectives John Shaw and Maurice Perkins—" The cameraman show the photos of the detectives. "—are suspected to be working for the infamous Phantom. For those who aren't familiar with Phantom, he's a mob boss-like figure that no one knows or has seen. But yet he is responsible for more than a hundred and seventeen deaths and the major distribution of narcotics in and around the Wisconsin area. Authorities say the investigation into the shooting death of 24-year-old Eric Wise has been ruled justified. It's said that Wise reached for something in his waistband and was shot eight times after giving an order to put his hands up. Both detectives are cleared of any wrongdoing and will return back to duty as early as tomorrow."

Fleetwood turned to Rome. "Friends of yours?"

"Friends? Nigga, you sound retarded. I don't know them pigs. And Rome ain't no friend of swine. I suspected the Phantom had to have some blue juice to make all them people disappear. Hearing them announce it on TV, I just had to see who it was he had behind him to make it happen."

Everyone began to make conversation with him about their own conspiracies about the Phantom and the police. Fleetwood hits the switch, turning the volume back to the music and off the TV. The song *The Payback* by James Brown blares through the speakers. Rome pretended nothing was wrong, but Fleetwood could tell something about seeing those cops on television knocked him off his square a bit. That wolf's smile wasn't on his face as it normally was when he was up to no good and Rome was always up to no good. So, he knew Rome had to be lying about knowing those cops. But the million-dollar question was why?

***

Rome walked into G's Clippers and was ritually greeted with respect and recognition from all in attendance. "My man G, get me tight and right for the Player's Ball, baby." Rome took a seat in his normal chair.

"I can't get you today, Rome. But this here is Polo." G points at Polo. "He's the new barber here and he's damn good. He's going to tighten you up today."

"G, you been my barber for over 15 years. Ever since you opened this place. And you've never tried to put me off on anyone else. So why take the sideline now?"

G showed him his right hand in a sling. "I was cleaning out the gutters on my house and fell off the ladder. I fractured my wrist. So, I'll be out of commission for a couple of months." The truth was G's favorite niece Peaches called in a favor to help Polo get closer to Rome.

"Damn, out of all the days of the year, you had to go and mess up yo golden hand on the day I need you the most. G, it's the Player's Ball, baby. And you want me to trust all this gorgeousness in the hands of a nigga I don't know?"

"Of course not. I want you to trust me. And I'm telling you this young player here has the Midas touch. Come on, baby, you know I won't drop a turd on your plate and tell you shit's sweet. Give him a try."

"G, I got mad love and respect for you. But if this nigga fucks me up, the both of y'all going to pay for that. Is that understood?"

"Completely." G turned to Polo and whispered to him, "Boy, you better do a damn good job because this is both of our asses on the line here."

"No worries, OG. I got this."

He leaned back in his chair and Polo prepped his bald head and face for a shave. "You look real familiar. I just can't pinpoint where I know you from. Polo you say your name is?"

Polo wrapped a hot towel around Rome's head and face. "Pimping Polo."

"Pimping Polo? You young cats kill me with your contradictive monikers. Niggas calling their selves shit like Killa Pete or Money Mike and ain't so much as killed a roach in their mama's kitchen or have more than a dime to their name."

"You don't have to worry about me being one of those cats. I plan to live up to mines." Polo removed the hot towels.

"Is that right? What could Polo the barber possibly know about pimping?"

"Everything you teach me."

"And that won't be much. I don't do the mentor thing. Check with Fleetwood or some of the other players in the game for that."

"If I wanted to know how to be number two or less then maybe I would've taken you up on that. I aim to be the best, so I come to the best. And I know for a fact you're not really going to turn me down." He ran the sharp straight razor down Rome's head, catching all the stray hairs and leaving a clean trail of skin.

"And what would make your monkey-humping ass think some shit like that?"

"A few reasons keeps me in the knowing of that. One, with you getting up there in age, no offense, you going to need someone you personally groomed and trust to takeover. And two, because I had a little talk with Sharon Wade."

"Sharon Wade?"

"Yeah, you remember Dimples, don't you?"

"The last time I seen ol' Dimples she had a crack pipe in her mouth and a trick's dick up her ass. That hoe used to bring me back a G or better a night. And now she's turning tricks in alleys for her next hit. Damn shame how such a good whore went to waste."

"Dimples used to be a bad little caramel thang back then, baby. And wasn't giving nobody but Rome the time of day. But I can't lie, when she got strung out on that shit, I had to pay her a visit. I had to put my spoon in that honeypot and see how good it was," Trick Child added.

"Was it as good as everybody say it was?" Tony Long asked him.

"Good enough to keep me coming back every Friday night for the last 9 years."

Everybody in the barbershop cracked up laughing.

"That's how you know Dimples, young stud? You played in them sugar walls and she told you how she used to be my whore and it gave you the ambition to want to be like me?"

Polo cleans the hair and shaving cream off the blade on a towel. "Nah, that would be incest considering Dimples is my mama."

The whole shop got quiet.

"You Dimples' boy?" Pimping Ball asked.

"Yeah. And she had some interesting stories to tell me, too, about my father."

"Who's yo pops?" Tony Swag asked from the chair next to Rome's while Finesse faded his hair.

"That's a funny story. She say she was messing with this cat when she got pregnant with me. He didn't want any kids by her because she was on that shit. So, he gave her money for an abortion. But instead of getting an abortion she went and got high. He never knew he had a son, and I never knew who my father was until just a few days ago. This story sound familiar to you, Rome? Or should I say pops?"

"You gotta be shitting me!" Rome moved Polo's hand from his face and took a long, hard look at him.

"It's like looking in the mirror ain't it?" Polo stared back.

"You telling us you're Rome's son?" Pimping Ball asked while being just as shocked as everyone else.

"What, y'all need a blood test or for me to call my mama and have her verify all that I'm saying?" Polo pulled out his phone.

Rome stared off in a daze as he looked at Polo. He couldn't believe it. He knew what Polo was saying was more than likely the truth. Dimples was pregnant by him. But because she was smoking crack, he didn't want her to have it. He didn't want to be the father of a crack baby even though he was the one responsible for Dimples becoming an addict.

He had gotten her hooked on powder to keep her amped up to get his money. A trick of hers introduced her to crack and she never looked back. Rome knew when she first started and could've stopped her then before she got too heavy on it. But he didn't give a fuck because she started hustling harder and could make his quarter and afford her high. When she got too bad on it, and beating and torturing her didn't make her quit, Rome cut her lose. Instead of addressing the issue everyone was dying for his opinion on, Rome rubbed his face as if he was trying to wipe the look of daze and shock off of it. "You want to finish my trim, young stud? I got a Player's Ball to attend."

Polo passed him a mirror. "I'm already done."

To his surprise Polo had done a better job than G had ever done on him. "I guess you were right, G. This player knows how to work a razor." Rome handed Polo a folded 50-dollar bill.

"I'm good. It's on the house."

"I don't need no favors. So put these frogs in your pocket." Rome slapped the money in Polo's hand. "Alright, I'll see you players tonight at the Player's Ball."

Polo felt something hard folded into the bill Rome had just given him. He opened it up to see Rome's business card.

Leaving the barbershop, Rome cruised over to Locust Street in search of Dimples. It didn't take him long to find her. She was standing outside of a corner store called Mother's on 16th Street, on the hunt for a dope date. Before he could turn the corner a rusted-out gold Regal pulled up on her.

She walked up to the car and leaned on its windowsill. "You looking to get one off, baby?"

"Oh, yeah, baby."

"What you got for me?" The man took a twenty out his wallet and held it out for her. She snatched the twenty and opened the car door.

Rome turned the corner and pulled in front of the car before Dimples could get in. He blew the horn then rolled down the front passenger window and held out a hundred-dollar bill.

Dimples closed the car door.

"Where you going?"

"Sorry, baby, but his money longer."

"Well, give me damn twenty back!"

"Here, you cheap mothafucka." Dimples balled the twenty up and threw it at him. Without looking at the driver Dimples seized the hundred-dollar bill and got into the car. She stretched the bill out and held it up to the sunlight to check its authenticity. "What you want, baby. Matter-of-fact, it don't even matter. You can do whatever you want to my body for this kind of money." Dimples looked at the driver for the first time. "Oh, shit it's you." She reached for the door, trying to get out, but Rome yanked her back. "What do you want, Rome?"

"Shut up, bitch. You know what I want. That boy of yours came by the barbershop and had a strange story to tell me."

"What do you want from me, Rome?"

"I want you to tell me that shit he was saying ain't true!" His eyebrows were furrowed and his face was so close to hers she felt the spit fly out his mouth when he spoke. She stayed quiet. Knowing Rome's temper, she didn't want to piss him off any further or that could mean a well whooped ass for her. "Bitch, that dick-sucker of yours better get to moving and words better get to coming." He raised his hand to her face. "Or it's going to be out of commission for a long time."

She covered her face with her hands and braced herself in case he struck her. "Okay, it's true! Polo is your son."

He knew if Dimples said he was his son it had to be the gospel. One thing he could say about that hoc was she could never lie to him. "You shysty whore. You have my child and I'm just finding out. That's some dirty shit."

"Coming from the man who does dirt like worms? You didn't even want me to have him, Rome."

"Because look at you. All cracked out and smoked up. Nothing like the woman you used to be. You wasn't fit to be nobody's mama. I wouldn't trust you to care of my dog let alone a child of mines."

"Think back at the man that you seen today. Did he look like a crack baby? No, because I was a good mother and took damn good care of him. And I never asked you for dime. Now, don't that contradict everything you thought about me being the mother of your child?" She was right. Polo didn't turn out too bad with her being his mother. Though he didn't want her to have him, a part of him was glad she did. He never had any kids and always wanted a son. Polo may be a grown man and Rome may have missed out on a lot in his life— things like teaching him how to ball, shave, drive and things like that. But it was still something he had left to teach him.

Chapter 7

The Rave club was packed almost to capacity. And still lines formed to almost around the corner with people trying to get in. Everyone wanted to attend the Player's Ball. Pimps pulled up in limos and extravagant rides with their whores and walked down the red carpet as the cameras flashed.

Rome and Fleetwood pulled up in a white Bentley limo with their women. As their limo drove off, a pink Rolls Royce stretched limo pulled up and out came Tweety and her team. She stepped out in a all-cotton candy blue colored Gucci pant suit with matching suit jacket. She wore no shirt underneath her suit jacket, exposing her beautiful yellow skin and her pink Gucci bra. Her team dressed in all cotton candy blue-colored shear Gucci dresses that exposed their pink Gucci bras and thong panties. The energy and excitement outside increased as they made their way down the red carpet. Sapphire hits the splits and shakes her ass and cameras flash wildly and the crowd gets geeked up. Giving the crowd a brief show before going inside made them want to get in there even more. Tweety looked over at Rome with a smile and winks before walking inside.

Rome turned to Fleetwood. "You took care of that business I told you to take care of?"

"I sure did. I even made her think I was on her side. She took the bait just like you said she would." Fleetwood passed Rome a little black book.

"Good, because like Big Hunnid said, this bitch gained a lot of game from Cadillac Bandz. I know this hoe is going to try and challenge me and I be damn if I lose the throne to a whore." Rome flips through the pages of the little black book. Satisfied with the contents inside he puts it inside coat pocket. The worry of losing the throne to Tweety wore deep on his mind. Because if he were to lose his crown to his ex whore, he would be an embarrassment to the game and the laughing stock of all the pimps and whores.

Inside the festivities were in full effect. Pimps adorned their bodies with the best and flashiest suits, minks and gators. Some took to the dancefloor with their women and others either chilled at their tables, chopped it up with the other pimps there, or shot game at the renegade whores in attendance.

Tweety and her team chilled at their tables in VIP, enjoying themselves and their drinks when Rome and Fleetwood walked over. "Ooh wee, look at here, Fleetwood. It's madam Tweety. Or should I say Pimping Tweety? Look a-there, she even has gator stilettos on."

"Well, you know I had to look my best on a night like this. I mean, it's a perfect night for a dethroning of a king, don't you think?"

"I highly doubt that would be achievable on your end. But it will be a pleasure to watch you try. You bitches enjoy y'all night." Rome tipped his hat towards them and walked off with Fleetwood by his side.

The whole club turned up when Slim Thug and Jazze Pha took the stage with their song *Everybody Loves a Pimp*. Tweety and her team took to the dance floor. The girls danced around her.

Princess, in the middle of having a good time took a step backwards and bumped into someone, nearly tripping over them. "I'm sorry." She collected herself. Then, as she looked up at the person, it was none other than Polo.

"No need to apologize for something that wasn't your fault. That was just life putting you exactly where you need to be. Right here with me."

Princess rolled her eyes. Slim Thug starts flowing his song *I Ain't Heard of That*, cranking the crowd up even more. "I don't think so. How did you get in here anyways?"

Polo straightened the jacket of his beige Gucci suit. "This is a Player's Ball isn't it? So why wouldn't this player be in attendance?"

It took everything in Princess to bite her tongue from telling him he was the farthest thing from a player. A player doesn't let his emotions control him and throw fits over a bitch he lost. A player doesn't destroy his product even if she was leaving him. Because a true player knows if his pimping is good, one day that hoe will come crawling back.

As Slim Thug exited the stage, Tweety hopped on and took possession of the mic. "Can I get everyone's attention please for a moment?" All eyes were on her, and seeing that she got everyone's attention, she continued. "I hope all you players and hoes out there are enjoying yourselves."

"We was until you got yo ass on stage!" Gator Red yelled out, trying to get a laugh.

"Nigga, shut the fuck up before I make your bottom hoe my footstool!" The crowd erupted into laughter. Gator Red sunk back into his seat, and she continued. "I'm not trying to kill no vibes. I'm up here to submit a formal notice of challenge to Rome for the throne in front of everyone."

Oohs and murmurs surfaced throughout the club and all eyes fell upon Rome who sat at his table with his hands stippled. The audience applauded as he got up and took to the stage. He gave Tweety a round of applause. A mic was brought out to him.

"I got to give it to you, baby. It takes a whole lot of woman to have the courage to come for the king. I would love to give these folks the opportunity to watch me embarrass your pretty ass as you try and take my crown." The crowd cheers him on. "But I can't." Disappointment surfs through the crowd. Rome pulls out the little black book. "You see, a pimp is not a whore and a pimp can't be challenged by a whore. By you still being an active whore—" Rome waves the little black book in the air before tossing it to Pimping Silky who was chairman of the board. "—you cannot be considered a pimp. That's the rules of the game."

Silky flips through Tweety's appointment book. "Tweety, I'm sorry, baby, but he's right. These dates show you are still active in the hoe game. Therefore, your challenge to Rome is invalid."

A huge grin creased Rome's face.

"Oh, I never said I was the pimp challenging Rome. My pimp is."

More murmurs surf through crowd.

"Your pimp?" Rome questioned, not knowing if he heard her right.

Her phone rings. She holds up one finger to Rome as she answered it. "Hello...? Okay... Everything's ready." She ended the phone.

Player Paul rushed in the club. "Y'all squares need to come outside. You won't believe this shit!"

"It seems like my pimp is making his entrance." Tweety spoke directly to Rome.

Everyone filed out the door. A marching band marched down the street playing Willie Hutch's song *I Choose You*. After the marching band was a carriage being pulled by four half-naked white whores. Tweety strolled to the curb and opened the carriage door. A cotton candy blue colored gator touched the concrete followed by its mate. People in the crowd looked over each other's shoulders trying to get a glimpse of the man who made such an entrance. The man that materialized shocked the whole crowd. He stood up with the help of his black and platinum cane with diamonds encrusted in its globe-shaped handle. His cotton candy pink ostrich skin Versace suit with matching Dobb hat and cotton candy blue silk shirt along with all his jewels showed the crowd his pimping was real. He snapped his fingers and the four white whores unharnessed themselves from the carriage and escorted him inside. The crowd parted when he walked past like Moses did the Red Sea.

"This shit can't be true," Rome said, thinking his thoughts out loud to Fleetwood.

"Oh, but it is. Boss is back from the grave, baby," Tweety told him as she walked past.

Isis stood in a state of shock when she saw him. Tears began to flow as she ran into his arms.

"Boss?" Princess left the much unwanted company of Polo.

Polo stood there with a look of utter confusion at seeing Boss still alive. But at the same time looking pissed that Boss's return interrupted the progress he thought he was making with Princess.

All his women crowded around him. "Boss, you're alive. How could this be? We seen the coroners remove your body from the car. We had your funeral and everything." Isis was full of questions.

"I know y'all have a bunch of questions and I'm going to break it all down to you later. First, I have some business to attend to."

"And you go handle that business." Tweety handed him a mic.

He took the mic and strolled away. "I know a lot of you thought I was dead and gone. But I'm here, baby. And tonight is the night I come for that crown." He stopped in front of Rome.

Rome looked over at Silky. "This can't be legit. A pimp must be active in the game to challenge a king. Having your mama handle yo pimping for you while you hide out doesn't count. A hoe must know who her pimp is and all your hoes believed yo mama to be their pimp."

"Actually Rome, there isn't a law against him pimping his mama to do his bidding. If his mama is his whore, then all that belongs to her belongs to him. Tweety, did you take all the proceeds from these hoes and give it to Boss?" Silky questioned.

"Every last dime."

"Then, that falls under the guidelines of pimping. I guess Rome you ain't the only nigga who can pimp their mama."

"Even if that wasn't sufficient enough, those four hoes that pulled my carriage in was out in here with me getting my money. I know you recognize three of them as the former whores of Fleetwood Slim. You see I never put my pimping on pause baby. Now if you are done trying to worm your way out, accept my challenge or forfeit the crown."

"Nigga I'm the king. I don't have to accept no challenge from you. I don't feel you are worthy enough."

"Actually Rome, to keep the crown you do." Silky interjected.

"What?"

"When you petitioned the council to add the law that only number two pimps could challenge the king, we accepted it with an added clause that if you fail to accept a challenge from number two that you will forfeit the crown making number two the new king."

"In other words, you have no choice but to accept my challenge." Rome got in Boss's face and stared him down.

"Fine. I accept your challenge!"

"But seeing that it ain't room in this game for the both of us, I say we raise the stakes. Whoever wins takes the crown but the loser is banished from the game for good."

Rome, not wanting to show weakness in front of everyone, agreed. The crowd got excited as they both took to the stage. A long table was set in front of the stage for the five council board members to sit and judge the event.

"Alright Rome, since you are presently the king you get to pick the challenge." Silky spoke.

"It ain't a challenge I can't beat him at. So let him choose his own means of punishment."

Oohs erupted from the audience.

"Okay, okay, balls in yo' court, Boss. What you choose pimp?"

"Let's do this ol' skool. I challenge you to a renegade round up."

"Oh now that's ol' skool for real. Alright for you squares that don't know what a renegade round up is let me explain. We take all the renegade hoes in the building and that's lined up outside and we bring them to the stage. The pimp that games and gains the most hoes wins the throne," Silky explained to the crowd. "Player Paul, go round up the renegades and let's get this show on the road."

Player Paul rushed off to round up the women. When he returned, he lined the stage with twelve beautiful whores. "Alright players, y'all know what time it is. Y'all have three minutes to spit your finest game to these twelve whores. Whomever gains the most hoes at the end wins the challenge and takes the throne." Silky holds up his watch and waits for the second hand to reach twelve. "Anddd… Go!" Rome and Boss, like savage wolves, attacked the women with vicious game.

The crowd cheered as Boss and Rome tried to press as many bitches as they could into submission. Silky kept an eye on his Rolex watching the three-minute time limit wind down. Polo stared at Princess from a far corner of the club. She didn't notice his eyes on her as her attention was on the stage. The longer he looked at her, the stronger his desire for her grew and the more he wanted to get rid of Boss to have her to himself again.

"Times up! Pimps step aside and let the ladies decide. Ladies walk to the man of your choice or walk off stage if you rather stay a renegade." Silky stepped over to the first girl in line. "Who you choose baby?" She walked off stage. The next girl stepped forward and walked over to Rome. The next four walked off stage. The next three walked over to Boss. Then two more walked onto Rome's team leaving one Asian girl left to break the tie. Rome glanced across the room at Polo and gave him a signal by rubbing his chin. Polo eased further back into the shadows. The Asian girl stepped forward and begin walking across the stage. Before the crowd could tell who side she was going to go to, shots rang out. Everyone rushed out of the club screaming and trampling over each other.

Boss raced over to his family to make sure they got out safe. When he looked over his shoulders, he seen Rome walking towards the front exit with a huge grin on his face. Boss knew then what was going on. It wasn't some random shooting. It was Rome's backup plan.

Chapter 8

Boss tucked Queenie into bed and kissed her on the forehead before closing the bedroom door and walking downstairs. Tweety and the girls sat around the dining room table. Boss took a seat at the head of the table. Sapphire played with the gold bracelet on her wrist, still in shock at what went down. "I can't believe somebody would have the audacity to shoot up a player's ball. Thank God nobody got hurt."

"This was Rome's doing."

Princess looked perplexed by his assumption. "Boss, how you figure? Rome was on stage with you when the shots ranged out."

"Of course he didn't pull the trigger himself but he had somebody do it. It was his backup plan. He got scared he was going to lose the challenge so he created a situation troubling enough to stop the challenge before I could win."

"Doesn't sound too farfetched. Trouble like this certainly has Rome's name all over it." Tweety chimed in.

"Now that that mystery is solved, you want to tell us how you rose from the dead black Jesus? Because I can't wrap my head around it." Gemini asked.

"Some things that don't make sense add up when you look back at them. When I left out the apartment I seen my driver's door open. I chirped the alarm and hit the remote start button to startle whoever was trying to break in the car. I didn't know the man was installing a bomb in it. So instead of the alarm scaring them off, it triggered the bomb and blew him up. He was burned so badly he couldn't be identified. I seen it as an opportunity to beat Rome at his own game. He wasn't going to stop coming for me until I was dead. I put my jewelry on the body then hid behind some bushes across the street. Princess dropped off mama's Escalade to me then jumped in the BMW with her and drove over to y'all. I figured I'd fake my death until the player's ball where he couldn't run and be forced to accept my challenge. But like the snake he is, he found a way to slither out of it." Boss slammed his fist on the table in frustration. No matter how close he gets to defeating Rome, Rome always finds a way to dodge his triumph.

"Wait a minute, you telling me the two of you knew he was alive this whole time?" Macita pointed her Twizzler in Tweety's and Princess's direction. They both nodded in agreement.

"It was mama's idea."

Macita then directed the conversation at Boss. "So, what do we do now?" She then took a bite of the Twizzler.

Boss got up from the table and picked up a small duffle bag off the China cabinet. He pours the contents out onto the table. The women stared down at all the guns that littered the table.

"Seeming him and I can't handle this shit like Ps." He picks up a nickel plated .45 and loaded a clip in it. "Then, I guess we got to handle it like Gs."

As much as Tweety wanted things to play out the player's way, she understood well that things had by then far pass being handled in a gentlemen's manner. Pistol play was then the only way to settle things. And Tweety was no stranger to gun play.

***

Peaches poured the men drinks and listened in on their conversation. "Somebody's deck of cards got a joker missing. Fleetwood you would have to be the biggest dummy in the crash test if you thought for one minute I wasn't going to have a plan B." Rome leaned back in his leather office chair and propped his feet up on his desk.

"How you suppose he faked his death."

"I don't know and don't care. All that matters is that bastard is still alive and still a problem."

"You say that with a smile like you're happy he's alive."

"What can I say Polo, the boy brings a certain amount of excitement to the game that I haven't experienced in a long, long time."

Peaches walked over and handed out the drinks. She stretched her eyebrows at Polo when she gave him his drink, signaling him to shoot his spill to Rome. He took big gulp of his drink and sat up straight in his chair.

"All fun and celebration to the side. I held my end of the bargain by shooting up the club and putting an early end to the challenge. It's time you hold up your end of the deal. Teach me your game."

"Patience my boy, patience. I'm going to teach you the game. But it's something I you got to explain to me first."

"What's that?"

"When I seen Boss in the club tonight and I looked over to give you the signal, it dawned on me where I knew you from. You're Boss's homeboy. You were with him that night we Charlied him."

Rome pulled out a chrome snug nose .38 from inside jacket pocket. He pointed the pistol center mass at Polo. "You better tell me what's going on real quick. Because son or no son, you plotting on me I'm gonna kill you." Polo sat calm, completely unnerved by the chrome reaper that stared at his chest. Peaches stood next to the bar across the room but her heartbeat could be heard thundering in her chest from where Polo sat.

"True, I was with Boss that night and even was his friend then. But that mothafucka don't mean shit to me now!" The devilish look in Polo's eyes gave strength to the wrath of his words against Boss. Rome still wasn't buying it. He cocked back the hammer on his pistol.

"Do it look like I jumped off a short yellow bus to you? You expect for me to believe you crossing your best friend for a father you don't know?"

"I believe you must've got off a short yellow bus if you believe that's the reason I'm going against Boss. I'm not doing this shit to be tight with you. I'm doing it because that bitch ass nigga played me. I had got my hands on a thoroughbred out of St. Louis. He was supposed to been putting me up on the game but instead he was plotting against me to take my bitch. Sadly, he succeeded."

"So you doing all this for a bitch?" Peaches' jealousy couldn't keep her mouth shut and remain a fly on the wall. Rome picked up his glass of scotch and threw it at her, striking her on the thigh. The thick scotch glass made a ting sound when it landed on the hardwood floor but didn't break. She yelp at the stinging pain and rubbed her aching thigh.

"Bitch stay the fuck out of grown folks business! And get yo' nosey ass up out of here!" Peaches limped out of the room. Rome uncocked his pistol and put it back in his jacket pocket. "Like father like son. That statement goes for us and them Bandz people. You know his father snaked me the same way. You don't need a psychology degree to understand I know exactly how you feel. That's why you want to learn the game. You want to steal his dreams of becoming king."

"I want the same thing you want. I want to kill any chance of him running this game. And I know just how to do it."

"I'm all ears." Rome listened closely while Polo broke down his plan to him. The plan was game loaded but it came with its dilemma. It was gonna take a lot of trust on Rome's end. Trust was something Rome didn't have much of for no one. The last person he trusted was Cadillac Bandz and that experience taught him to fuck all and trust none. Though it was clear to him if he wanted to get rid of Boss, he was gonna have to trust the closest helping hand. So, he gave in to the plan.

Chapter 9

Tony Swag and Pimping Ball scrolled up and down the track on foot in search of some new women to add to their stables. It was a lame night out on the tracks. Most Mondays were. Tricks were returning back to work after the weekend and going straight home to their families. Though it was always those few stragglers out lurking for some action before returning home. By there being a lot of down time for the hoes on a night like that, Pimping Ball and Tony Swag were able to spot all the new faces on the track.

"The hoe got to running her mouth, right? So I tell her, a good hoe don't talk, they listen bitch. Now get your ass on and click them heels and get my bills."

"Tony Swag you gon' lose that bitch before you check a decent bag out her."

"What? Take a look at me, Pimping Ball. I'm fine as wine and got hoes dying for my time." Tony Swag opened his Armani jacket and spun around. "Mane, listen here, that bitch would rather walk through a lion's den with a pork chop skirt on than to ever leave me. I'm the greatest thing to happened to that bitch since she came out her mammy's ass."

The walked into a restaurant on the corner of 3rd and Mitchell. They took a window seat with a view of the busy street. They both flipped through the menu as they conversed. "You went to see the Phantom the other day didn't you, Ball?"

"I wouldn't necessarily say I seen him. After all these years, I've never seen that man's face. All I ever seen of him was his shadow."

"The same here. Every time I go meet with him it's in a strange place where he could see me but I couldn't see him."

"I know what you mean. One time, he made me meet with him at a Black Lives Matter protest. I marched for hours before he had told me to veer off onto another block. When I did, a man in a mask on a motorcycle zoomed passed and snatched the bag out my hand. Then, the Phantom texted me and told me I could go home."

The overweight waiter came over to their table breathing hard from the short walk over. He collects their orders. They hand him their menus and he wobbles off to get their orders.

"That's one mysterious nigga. What did he have to say about what went down at the Player's Ball?"

"Not much. He said as long as Rome keeps his ass planted on that throne and nothing interferes with business than he really don't give a fuck."

"You think Rome ever seen his face?"

"I know he had to have seen his face. Rome's the closest person to the Phantom. It's no one else the Phantom would trust. Why you think he won't let him leave the throne."

"There just might be some truth in what you saying."

The waiter returns to the table forehead raining sweat and wheezing like an asthmatic. He sat their pizza and drinks down on the table.

"Can I get you gentlemen anything else?" He spoke in a heavy Spanish accent that let them know English was barely even a secondary language to him.

"You can get the hell away from my food with all that sweating." Pimping Ball covered the food with his hands.

"And while you at it, hook yourself up to an oxygen tank before you pass out in here."

The waiter walked off mumbling something in Spanish.

"What do you make of Boss faking his death and showing up at the player's ball?"

"Pure game!" Tony Swag broke off a slice of pizza and sprinkled Parmesan cheese on top of it.

"The nigga was running scared. Rome had that nigga so spooked he faked his death. You call that game?"

"You looking at from the wrong angle. Analyze his game under this lens. True enough, Rome was at his head. But Rome was also dodging him. Boss found a way to kill both of those birds with one stone. The nigga recruited his own mama and used her as a diversion. Then stepped to Rome at the player's ball leaving him no room to run. And throughout the whole process, he was still getting his money. Like I said, pure game." Tony Swag took a bite of his pizza.

"If you say so. But if we were to measure things out on an overall scale, Boss game ain't fucking with Rome's."

"To each man his own opinion." Tony Swag dropped his pizza back down on his plate when something outside caught his attention. "Say, ain't them Rome's girls right there?" He pointed at Ashley and Hannah.

"Damn sho is."

"What in the world them hoes doing walking the track? That's white gold, you sell that shit online not the streets."

"Rome probably punishing them bitches for some type of insubordination. You remember how Cadillac used to do his bitches when they would fuck up or not meet his quarter?"

"Yeah, make the bitch work the track until she could appreciate the comforts of working online. Well if that's what Rome's going for with them, then I'm quite sure his scared straight program will work out just fine with their preppy asses."

"Damn straight. After dealing with the tricks out here, turning dates in cars instead of comfortable hotel beds, by the end of the night them bitches going to be begging Rome to forgive them and take them back in doors."

An Escalade pulled up beside Hannah and Ashley. Gemini and Sapphire stepped out of the truck and approached them. "Y'all hoes a long way from home, ain't y'all?" Sapphire held her hands behind her back as she came toward Hannah. Hannah turned around. Seeing who it was she adjusted her purse on her shoulder with one hand then slipped the other one inside it to grip her blade.

"That's the perks of America. It's a free country. Meaning, we can go wherever we please."

"That sound real patriotic and all but that don't mean you ain't got to pay taxes when you step on certain turfs. And this is one of those turfs where you going to have to pay." Ashley stepped forward.

"We're not paying you two shit!" Gemini snatched her by the hair.

"Bitch if we say y'all are y'all are and it's nothing neither of you can do about it."

"Oh yeah?" Hannah swiftly brought out her switch blade. She hit the switch causing the blade to pop up. "Back the fuck off!" Gemini and Sapphire looked at each other and laughed.

"You hoes in the hood and y'all depending on a switch blade for y'all protection?" Sapphire took her hands from behind her back revealing 9mm Beretta. Gemini brought out its twin, aiming it at Ashley's head. Hannah and Ashley screamed and hung onto each other in fear.

"Scream all you want to. That shit is like music out here. Don't nobody give a fuck and the police don't come these ways."

Hannah and Ashley got even more terrified.

"Now, you bitches run that dough." They both tossed their purses over to them. Gemini picked them up. She counted the money in both purses, $475. "We'll take the rest of the money y'all stashing."

"That's all we have. We only been out here an hour."

"Ashley, boo boo ain't written on our foreheads. Did you forget we're hoes too? We know you got money stashed on you and we know you two been out here for three hours. We been watching y'all."

"She's not lying! That's all the money we have!"

"Hannah are the two of you really going to make us go there?" Neither of them said anything. "Fine, have it y'all way." Gemini fired three shots at their feet making them scream and hop around in place. "Strip! Take it all off! Now!"

Shaking into tears, they shredded their clothes from their bodies as quick as they could. "Squat and cough!" They did as they were told. Sapphire searched their clothes.

"Bingo!" She found their stash in makeshift pockets inside their bras. She counted $850. "Gemini, we out." Sapphire and Gemini still with their guns trained on them treaded back to the truck.

"Give us our clothes back!"

"Not in this lifetime. Look at it this way, I'm helping your hustle. The less clothes you wear out here the more tricks that will stop for you."

"You hoes have fun making y'all way back to the suburbs." Gemini and Sapphire laughed and smashed off in the Escalade leaving Hannah and Ashley naked and huddled together.

Pimping Ball and Tony Swag stared out the window with their jaws dropped. "Ball, did you just see that shit?"

"Wasn't that Gemini and Sapphire?"

"Yeah that was them."

"And ain't they Boss's bitches now?"

"Yup."

"Rome ain't going to like this one."

"I think you better call him."

"I'm calling him now." Pimping Ball dialed up Rome and explained to him what had just occurred then ended the call.

"That brother pissed. I could hear his voice cracking the speaker of the phone. What was he saying though?"

"Basically, that Boss cut into his last nerve. They called him from some trick's phone while we were talking. He's on his way down here. He want us to keep an eye on them until he gets here."

"Nigga please, who I look like Mary Poppins? I ain't babysitting no hoe that ain't mine."

"You right about that. Let's get out here and see if we can catch those Mexican bitches that's selling ass by the gas station." Tony Swag wiped his mouth then threw the napkin in his plate. The waiter wobbled over to clean off their table as they got up to leave.

"Amigos, no tip?" He held his small fat sweaty hand out to them. Pimping Ball picked up a slice of pizza then slapped it onto his hand face down splattering sauce all over his hand.

"There you go my fat friend. Don't eat all at once."

The waiter cursed them out in Spanish as they left out laughing.

Chapter 10

The sun shined high above the horizon. Sea eagles screeched as they circled the air above the lake and swooped down to snatch up fish. Two couples played volleyball on the beach. Other people sprinkled on the beach, laid around tanning enjoying the sun, walking or playing Frisbee. Boss, Isis and Queenie was amongst those that walked the beach. He pushed Queenie along in her wheelchair. She still couldn't walk or talk but Boss could tell she understood everything going on around her.

They got some ice cream from a nearby vendor then cop a squat on a bench in front of the water. Isis swirled her tongue around her ice cream cone and watched as Boss spoon fed Queenie a chocolate sundae. It was something she needed to tell him. Something she had been keeping from him and for good reason. But she didn't know if she told him he would understand her reasoning. She was also afraid of him finding out on his own and resenting her for not telling him herself. Being the ex-woman of his enemy, she was barely in the realm of his trust as it was. After everything that was going on and the phone call she got the other night, she felt it was time she let Boss in on her secret.

"Daddy, I need to tell you something."

"Is it about you constantly sneaking off to meet up with Pimping Ball and Tony Swag throughout the week?" Boss kept his attention on feeding Queenie as he spoke. Isis was shocked with surprise. She didn't know his eyes that close on her.

"You know about that?"

"Them niggas ain't serving me no notice saying they peeled you from me. My money ain't been short. So either Pimping Ball and Tony Swag tricking off on you on the low or you trying to double cross me with Rome."

"Nah, I swear it's not at all what you're thinking."

Boss turned his head in her direction with a scowling look on his face. "Then, you better give me a good enough reason to why a bitch of mines is meeting up with other pimps."

She felt her ice cream start to melt down her hand and chucked it into the lake. Two sea eagles fought as they both dove for it. She took a baby wipe out her purse wipe to her with.

"I make runs."

"What do you mean you make runs?"

"You heard of the Phantom, right?"

"What about him?"

"Rome and a few other pimps Rome handpicked works for him. It's no secret the Phantom runs the drug trade in Wisconsin. But what people don't know is that he uses pimps and not drug dealers to push his product. And the pimps use their top hoes to push the product to the dealers for them."

"Why would do he use pimps instead of dope boys?"

"Because most of the dope dealers are under the watchful eye of the feds. A pimp sends his bitch and the feds don't suspect nothing more than the niggas buying some pussy. I pick up product from Pimping Ball and Tony Swag, off it to the dealers and drop the money back off to them."

"My next question. You're not with Rome anymore. Why the fuck his you still hustling for him?" The death stare he gave her was threatening. But guilt held more presence than fear in Isis at the moment.

"I tried to quit. Then, I had got a call the other night reminding me why I couldn't. I have no choice. If I don't, the

Phantom will have me killed. He knows everyone Rome has in play dealing with this operation. No one can be added to the business without Rome getting the Phantom's authorization first. Anyone who leaves or speak of his operation gets zipped up, body bagged. If I quit, he may even come for you to get to me. Don't you see Boss, I'm trapped in this shit." The weight of her predicament on her mind showed with the bags that were forming under her eyes. She hadn't slept much since that phone call.

"I'm going to get you out of this shit. Even if I got to kill the Phantom myself."

"Boss, you can't be seriously talking about taking out the Phantom."

"Why wouldn't I go after any man that's threatening my money, my livelihood?"

"For one thing, no one but Rome knows who the Phantom is. And nobody puts the fear of God in Rome more than the Phantom. So, he'll never expose the Phantom's true identity to anyone."

"Maybe he'd change his mind if his life depended on it."

"I doubt it."

"I don't. You and I both know Rome's the biggest self-centered bastard on the planet earth. If it's one thing I know about people like that is they'll do whatever it takes to protect their own self-interest. Even if that meant facing their fears."

"I'm not following."

"Dig, you say you know how the whole operation work, right?"

"Yeah."

"Then you going to run down every single detail of it to me. Rome ain't got to reveal who the Phantom is. We going to trap ourselves a snake to bait a vulture."

"Whatever you say, daddy." Isis felt horrible about having to keep such a secret like that from him. A secret that could possible put his life in danger if Rome or the Phantom had any inkling that she told him about their operation. True, she was taking a major risk now by telling him, but with all the drama going on that's threatening his life, she wanted him to be aware of what else he was up against. She just hoped whatever Boss had planned was enough to put an end to all the drama and keep them safe in the process.

They sat there for the next twenty minutes as Isis broke down every detail of the operation to him. Boss listened intently then told her what he wanted her to do to put his plan in play. When the conversation was finished, they got up and began walking back to the car.

They stopped for Boss to tie Queenie's shoes. "Boss, you wiped all her lip gloss off when cleaned that ice cream off her mouth." Isis dug into her purse for her lip gloss.

Isis and Queenie wasn't friends but Isis kept things between them cordial to appease Boss. Plus, she felt awful about Queenie's condition.

Isis got lip gloss and was ready to apply it to Queenie's lips but paused when she seen the look on her face. Queenie was frowned up and breathing heavily. "No need to get upset. If you don't want me touching you, I won't." Isis took a step back from her and held her hands up. Boss looked up at Queenie. Isis thought Queenie was reacting to her but Boss could see Queenie's attention was drawn to something behind her. Not wanting to be caught slipping, his hand reached under Queenie and rested on the Glock 17 he had stored under her lap. On the chrome armrest of the wheelchair, Boss watched the reflection of the man coming towards them. The closer the man came, the tighter his grip got on the Glock and the more he pulled it out from under Queenie.

When the man reflection became more than a blurry figure in the chrome, Boss could make out who it was. And the familiar face didn't ease his tension much.

"Big Boss hog. It's funny running into you here." Boss folded the towel, he used to clean Queenie's face, over the gun. With the gun concealed under the towel in his hand, he stood up to face Polo.

"I can't recall the last time I seen you just taking a scroll down the lakefront. So, forgive me Polo if what you saying right now sounds like bullshit to me."

"I was just enjoying the beach breeze with my new hoe bitch, Kiwi." Polo wrapped his arm around a thick redbone with rainbow colored hair and hazel eyes.

"I'm sure you were. By the way, congratulations on finding your father. I hear the two of you been kicking it real close."

"Perhaps you could say were making up for lost times. It turns out we have a few things in common."

"I could only imagine what things that could be." Queenie's breathing became erratic. Boss thought she was going to have a panic attack. "Isis, take Queenie to the car. I'll be there in a minute." Isis took control of the wheelchair. Queenie's face was scowling hard at Polo as Isis pushed her away.

"She didn't look to happy to see me."

"Maybe because the last time she remembers seeing you, you had beat Princess to a bloody pulp. Then, you turned on me thinking I was trying to steal her from you."

"She's with you now ain't she?" Boss broke eye contact for a brief moment. To Polo that showed his guilt. "It doesn't matter, it's all water under the bridge. Say we leave the past in the past and let bygones be bygones?" Polo held his hand out.

Boss looked down at it, sure it was some kind of trick to his peace offering. Princess had already told him Polo was trying to push up on her at his funeral. That alone let Boss know Polo wasn't really over her. But longing to have his best friend by his side again he ignored all red flags and accepted his hand of peace.

"I'm with that." As he shook his hand and looked at the wolfish smile on his face, he couldn't help but feel the handshake was the roofie in his drink before being fucked.

"Yo' I got to split and get this hoe back on the hustle. But I'm glad we can make a amends. See you at the Player's Picnic?"

"I'll be there."

Polo walked off with Kiwi under his arm. Boss waited for them to be out of his sight before he turned his back and left. He may have let Polo back into his life but it didn't mean he trusted him. Especially knowing the close relationship him and Rome shared. As the old adage goes, keep your friends close and your enemies even closer. Boss wasn't sure just yet which category Polo fell in so he was going to treat him like a friend and keep him closer than an enemy.

Chapter 11

The dining room table was adorned with smothered chicken, rice, cornbread, fresh steamed carrots and a pitcher of lemon iced tea. It was Tweety's normal routine of making Sunday dinner.

"Umm mm, I tell you Tweety, you never seem to disappoint my appetite every Sunday. You got it looking and smelling like a fat man's heaven in here." Aaron loaded his plate with food.

"He ain't lying mama. I can starve all week and get fat on Sunday." Tweety leaned over and Boss kissed her on the cheek. Then, he shook out some hot sauce onto his smothered chicken and sprinkled sugar on his rice. The chief slapped his hand on Boss's back.

"Boss, I'm so glad to see you still with us. I almost lost it when I seen that body that we suspected was yours. I wish you y'all would've told me the truth. I could've helped you."

"Chief, you doing enough. Did you find out who the guy was that was planting the bomb?"

"He was burned too bad to get fingerprints so we had to go through dental records to get an ID on him. The records ID him as being 49 year old Anthony Hack. He went by the moniker Boom. You know him?"

Boss thought hard on the name but it didn't ring a bell to him. "Can't say I do. Who is he?"

Tweety poured herself a glass of tea then refilled the chief's glass. The chief concentrated on devouring his meal as he continued talking.

"An ex-demolition worker turn meth head. His record showed he'd been arrested numerous times for drug possession. A confidential informant told us he was using his explosive expertise to gain employment with some real shady type of employers. One of those shady characters he was known to occasionally worked for was Rome." The chief paused eating to catch the reaction on Boss's face to what he had just revealed to him. "You don't look shock."

Boss's face showed no surprise. The chief only confirmed what he and his mama suspected all along. "Why would I be? The guy was a worm. Rome is the biggest worm I know. And all the worms around here dig the same dirt. No surprise, they did dirt together."

A hell of a way to look at it."

The doorbell rang.

"I don't know who that could be." Tweety wiped her mouth and got up to answer the door.

She opened the door surprise to see Fleetwood standing there. "Fleetwood, what brings you by here?" She welcomed him in and closed the door behind him.

"I needed to stop by and put this bug in your ear." He followed her into the dining room. He was taken off guard when he seen Boss and the chief sitting at the table. "I didn't know you had company. I can stop by another time."

"Nonsense, pull up a chair and fix yourself a plate." Boss pointed at an empty chair across from him. Fleetwood thought about it a moment before he took a seat. Things were straight between him and Tweety but him and Boss situation had yet to been confronted. For Fleetwood the beef between them was dead but he didn't know if Boss's mind was in the same place. To be safe, under the table his hand rested on his .25 that he sat on his lap when he sat down.

The chief stood up from the table rubbing his belly. Then he stretched his arms and yawned. "Well, let me get on home and get some sleep. I got a long shift to look forward to tomorrow. Y'all have a nice day. Angela, like always thanks for that delicious meal."

"You know you're always welcome, Aaron. See you next Sunday?"

"You can bet on it."

"Later chief." He waved bye to Boss and walked out the door.

Fleetwood forked two drumsticks onto his plate of rice. "My mama tells me you're quite the ally for us lately. I tell you, I wasn't too convinced you really switched teams. I told her you had to be playing spy games." Boss leaned back in his chair. His hands were under the table. It made Fleetwood nervous and clutch his deuce five tighter. "Then, she told me that she gave you all the evidence you needed to show you that it was Rome that set you up and not me. Revenge is a strong enough reason to make any man switch sides." Boss raised his glass to toast to Fleetwood. "Good to have you as an ally pimp." Fleetwood toasted glasses with him.

"I just want to ensure that mothafucka Rome gets the pain he got coming."

Tweety came back and sat down after clearing the chief's dishes from the table.

"Trust and believe he will. Now what's this bug you say you want to put in my ear?"

"Remember when I called you and told you I found out Polo was Rome's son?"

"I remember that."

"That shooting at the player's ball was all their plan. Rome and Polo made a deal. Rome wanted him to shoot up the club to end the ball if he felt like he was going to lose the challenge. Rome told him if he did that he would teach him all he knew about the game." Boss looked over at his mama.

"I told you it was all his doing. I'm not the least bit shocked that Polo was in on it either."

"But that's not all. Polo came by the day after the player's ball. He had something he wanted to run by Rome. It was a plan to get rid of you."

"What was the plan?"

"That part I don't know. Polo wanted to keep that between him and Rome. They expelled me from the room before they even began to discuss it. All I can tell you is it's something major. My advice is be aware of any and everything around you. I don't know much about Polo but if he's anything like his father, then the two of them together could only spell hell on earth." The sound of a glass bottle rolling into the metal gate outside the dining room window interrupted the conversation. All three of them jumped on point. Tweety went for her purse for her Glock. Fleetwood gripped his pistol. Boss pulled a black .45 from the small of his back and went to the window. He took cover from the side of the window and peeped out.

"What is it?" Tweety whispered over to Boss from the kitchen entrance.

"I don't see anything. Must've been a stray cat or something on the side of the house." Tweety and Fleetwood both relaxed and put their guns away.

"That probably was a sign for me to split. I don't want Rome to catch me here with y'all. We all know how bad that would be."

"Alright. Let me wrap your plate up for you."

Tweety restocked Fleetwood's plate and sent him on the way.

"Mama I'm gonna roll out too." Boss gave her a kiss.

"See you later baby. Take that trash out for me on your way out."

"I got you." He gathered the trash then left out the backdoor. He opened the raggedy green garbage can and two squirrels flew out, scaring him. He dropped the garbage bag and pulled out his gun. The squirrels chased each other up a tree making squeaking noises. Boss chuckled at himself and put his gun back in the small of his back. He threw the bag of garbage into the raggedy green can then treaded to his car. He stopped on the side near the dining room window. He looked down and seen a fresh pair of boot prints in the mud under the window.

His mama's house was compromised. Whoever was outside the window intentions couldn't been any good. He didn't want to take any chances on them harming his mama. He had no choice but to get her out of there.

He had her pack everything she needed and move into his house. That way he could keep her safe in his gated community.

***

The man ran to his car around the block. He worked hard to catch his breath while he dialed Rome's number. Rome picked up immediately.

"Yeah."

"I was outside of Tweety's house listening in on an interesting conversation between her, Boss and your main man, Fleetwood."

"Fleetwood? You sure?" Curiosity sank in Rome's mind before anything else. He couldn't think of any legitimate answer as to why Fleetwood would be over there.

"I know what I heard and who I seen. I hid in the alley and watched him come out the house."

"What was he talking to them about?" It was hard for Rome to believe that Fleetwood would have the balls to cross him.

"He was warning them that you and that son of yours have something big planned against them. He didn't know what though. He also told them about how the two of you caused the early end of the ball. You need to take care of this mess,

Rome. This shit is becoming a major problem and is bad for business."

"Oh, don't worry, I'm going handle Fleetwood."

"It's not just Fleetwood Phantom, it's this whole thing with you and the Bandz family. We got a shipment of fifteen kilos coming in the day before the player's picnic. I plan on collecting my money the day of with no problems. If there is any problems, well I don't have to remind you what happens when my money is played with, do I?"

"No sir."

"Good. Make sure that bitch Isis makes her drop offs and collects on time."

"Will do." The Phantom hung up the phone and drove away.

Chapter 12

All eyes was on Polo as he cruised down Capitol Drive blowing a blunt of loud in his new Chameleon painted Range Rover. "Slatt Zy's song, Heart Right," banged through the speakers. The truck sat high on 28 inch chrome Rucci rims.

Kiwi reached over and turned the music down. "Damn, can I hit that blunt?"

Polo reached into his boxers and pulled out half an ounce of loud and tossed it over to her. "Roll your own."

"Why I can't just hit yours?"

"I don't kiss whores and I don't smoke after them neither. It's blunts in the armrest."

"Stop playing and let me hit that." Her hand started to reach for his blunt. He grabbed her wrist. His eyes cut into her like daggers putting her every motion on pause. "You think I'm a game bitch, play me. You touch this blunt and I'm going to put your head through that window." He pushed her hard away from him causing her to bump her head on the window.

She made a hissing noise and rubbed the sore spot on her head. She searched Polo's face for any sign of remorse. There was none there. He continued puffing on the blunt as he drove like nothing had happened. She opened the armrest, grabbed the blunts out of it and began to roll her own smoke. "I bet you wish you would've done that at first. Because if you did your head would've be hurting right now." He chuckled and took a pull of the loud.

Rome had been putting Polo on to the guerrilla pimping game. Rome told him the truest pimp is the guerrilla pimp. A guerilla pimp has no sweet emotions for a hoe. His soul is as cold as the iceberg that sank the Titanic. The only way to be to have a hoe's respect is to make her fear to fail you. Everything Rome's been teaching him he'd been practicing on Kiwi and Peaches. The outcome of his practices been showing him that his father was indeed the truth. He had both of them in line like geometry. Guerilla pimping brought out Polo's dark side and it felt good to him.

He made a right on Atkinson Street then another right on 11th Street. He drove a couple blocks south to 11th and Keefe Street. The truck came to a stop in front of Kiwi's sister Charmaine's house, a brown and white duplex five houses from the corner. Kiwi's four year old son, Cairo played cops and robbers with Charmaine's two boys in the front yard. Benny, Charmaine's baby daddy was barbecuing and sharing a bottle of Amsterdam with three of his homies standing out there with him. He seen Polo pull up and dropped what he was doing.

"Here comes this bitch ass nigga." Polo smacked his lips and rolled down his window.

Benny was a certified chump. He pretended in front of his boys to be bigger than what he really was. The truth was he was a petty weed hustling nigga that was a confidential informant for Detective Shaw and Perkins. The bitch nigga snitched on half the niggas in the hood. Kiwi gave Polo the whole scoop on him.

Benny came over to Polo's side of the truck. His eyes worshipped the Range Rover. "Okay, big money doing big things. I see how you living Polo."

"Don't let your eyes fool you. What you see is all on credit. I'm just a poor man trying to make poverty look good."

"Sure you are." Polo noticed Benny's eyes fall upon the platinum chain around his neck and diamond pinky ring on his finger. He quickly moved his hand off the windowsill of the truck and clinched his chain.

"A little something from my pops." Charmaine came out the house in some shorts that hugged her butt cheeks. Benny's homeboys checked out her ass on the low as she came down the porched steps and walked towards Kiwi's side of the truck.

Charmaine looked like Doja Cat and had ass for days. She was older than Kiwi by three years. Every nigga in the hood been trying to smash her. Though some major ballers came close but no cigar. She knew niggas in her hood were worse than bitches and liked to talk. She was afraid of Benny finding out. Benny knew she was out of his league. He had gotten her pregnant on purpose by switching her birth control with vitamin pills. It was his pathetic way of putting her on lock before she found out he wasn't the baller he pretended to be to get her. Sadly, it worked. She was stuck with him. It wasn't love on her end, it was entrapment.

"Benny, your barbeque burning."

"Oh shit!" Benny rushed over to attend to the food on the grill.

"Charmaine, I need you to watch Cairo for me for a few days while I go out of town."

"No, no, no. No way. Cairo my nephew and all but I got my own kids to be watching." Charmaine watched Polo pull out a fat knot of bills from the pocket of his St. Laurent jeans. Seeing all that money made her pussy wet. He peeled three hundred dollars off his bankroll and held it out to her.

"This should make up for the next three days of inconvenience."

"Is Benny looking this way?" Kiwi looked passed her and seen Benny was watching her. Benny wasn't a pimp. He was just a glorified babysitter that stole every dime she got her hands on so he could party with his buddies.

"You know he is."

"Slip it in my titties." Charmaine leaned forward putting her big titties on display and blocking Benny's view. Kiwi got the money from Polo. Charmaine gave Polo a seductive look as Kiwi slipped the money between her titties and into her bra. It wasn't news to Polo that Charmaine wanted him. Little did she know, he wanted her. But he wasn't going to chase her like most niggas did. He didn't need her to just desire him. He needed her to crave him. Once she breaks that threshold of wanting him to needing him then he would make his move on her.

"You better go back over there by your man before he get a crook in his neck." Kiwi passed Charmaine her makeup mirror. She looked in the mirror and seen Benny trying to strain his neck to see what she was doing. She exhaled a heavy breath, snapped the mirror close before handing it back to Kiwi and walking off.

"Hurry up and pack your bag. I want to get out of here before traffic gets too heavy." Kiwi got out the truck, Cairo rushed over to her. She picked him up giving him a hug and kiss. Then she sat him back down.

"Go play, mama got to go okay?"

"Okay." Cairo ran off shooting a cap gun at his cousin. Kiwi walked sassily towards the porch to show off in front of the niggas outside. Polo leaned over and yelled out the passenger window. "Bitch stop trying to cute and get yo' whack ass in the house and do what the fuck I told you!" The intensity of his voice made her jump. Kiwi put a little more pep in her step. Charmaine along with everyone else outside laughed at her.

Kiwi and Charmaine's little brother, Desmond came out the house as Charmaine was going in. Desmond joined Polo inside the truck. They shook hands when he got in. "You killing the city with this ride, bruh." Desmond rubbed his hand across the dashboard.

"It's aight. Bigger and better things are on the way for us little, bruh."

"For us?"

"Yeah little nigga. You think I'm going to climb to the top and leave you at the bottom? That's not how I get down. I want you to be my right hand man."

"Polo, the pimp game ain't my choice of play."

"I know, you too gangsta for that shit. I'm not making any effort of taking you out of your field. In fact, I got some shit I'm putting together that's right up your alley."

Desmond was only seventeen but had the heart of a G. Polo seen that when he first met him and Kiwi. One day Polo was driving in the truck that Princess gave him delivering some weed to a customer on the north side. He stopped at a light on 35th and Vilet Street and before he knew it Desmond had come running from the side of the Check Cashers building with a gun in his hand and jumped into his backseat. Some niggas was running up the block after him with guns. He quickly tossed a hundred dollar bill at Polo and told him to get him out of there. Polo didn't know him from Adam or Eve but judging by the big knot Desmond was clutching tight in his hand, he knew he had just robbed the niggas that was at his head. Polo tossed him back the hundred and drove him home anyway. When he dropped him off, Desmond introduced him to his sister Kiwi. It didn't take much for him to game her. She was the neighborhood jump down. Polo was impressed with Desmond. He respected his gangsta and knew one day it would come in handy for him.

"What you talking?"

"I'm talking a lot money. But you might have to exercise your trigger fingers a little."

"You ain't talking nothing I ain't with. I may not be a pimp but you know I love to put my bitches to work." He held up two black .45's with woodgrain handles. "Just tell me the lick and who to hit."

"I'ma let you know when the time come. First, I got to hit this shit with a little finesse. Butter a mothafucka up to get them to slipping. You know what I mean?"

"No doubt."

Kiwi came out the house with a small traveling bag. She gave Cairo a kiss goodbye then made her way towards the truck.

"Look here hot boy, I need you to keep it cool until we make this move, aight?"

Kiwi put her bag in the trunk.

"I'ma try, I can't make no promises. Bro a mothafucka got to eat out here."

Polo pulled his money out and handed Desmond two G's. "That should hold you until we bust that move."

Kiwi opened the passenger front door. "Desmond get yo' ass out so we can go."

"Shut yo' ass up. He'll get out when he feel like it. Close the door and stand yo' ass out there until we done talking."

She closed the door and leaned against a tree with her arms folded across her chest.

"You just bought me a chill pill. You got my word, I'll stay smooth. Just make sure we catch that cheese sooner than later. Two Gs don't last forever."

"It won't be long. Now get yo' ass up out of here so I can put your sister to work." They shook hands. Desmond exited the truck and Kiwi got in. Charmaine with a flirtatious smile waved bye to Polo. Kiwi seen it.

"Thirsty bitch," she whispered to herself then rolled the window up to conceal Charmaine's view of him behind the limo 5% tint. With his final piece on the chessboard in position, Polo turned the music up and peeled off the block ready for the battle that was going to take place.

Chapter 13

Boss walked into a small blues joint on the north side of town. Johnny Taylor's song, Jody's Got Your Girl And Gone, played on the jukebox. The bar held a nice size crowd of men and women that was old enough to be his parents or grandparents. The women made passes at him and eyed him like he was a sweet piece of candy that they couldn't wait to get in their mouths. Cigarette and cigar smoke made clouds throughout the bar. Through the fog of smoke, Boss was still able to make out his uncle Big Hunnid sitting at the bar. Big Hunnid wore a maroon leather jacket with a tan colored Fedora hat. He was smoking on a cigarette and listening to Sugar Shack talk his ear off. Sugar Shack dressed like a ol' skool pimp but was a well-known trick. Sugar Shack probably tricked off on half the veteran whores in the game. He was known to talk a mile away when he got too much Crown Royal and wine in his system. He thought he was Confucius or somebody the way he kicked his whacked out philosophies.

Boss took a seat next to Big Hunnid.

"What's going on, Unc?"

Big Hunnid cut his eyes Boss's way. "I seen that pretty Rolls Royce of yours traveling up Vine Street earlier. It's good to see it was that Benz that blew up and not the Wraith."

"It's better that I didn't blow up, don't you think?"

"That's good news too."

"Hey, is that Boss on the other side of you?" Sugar Shack asked.

"What's going on Sugar Shack?"

"Oh, you want me to tell you something?"

"Hit me with some of that homegrown wisdom of yours."

"Let me tell you something Boss. You know what is the greatest thing in this world besides money and power to a trick?

"What's that ol' skool? "

"Cookies and pussy." He held up a chocolate chip cookie for Boss to see.

"Cookies and Pussy?"

"Cookies and mothafuck'n pussy! Their synonymous. Listen good and I'm going to tell you why. Peep game, a cookie is the representation of a whore. It's round shape reminds him of how pussy makes his world go round. Just like a cookie's sweet, delicious taste is bad for his health and a whore is bad for his marriage, he still eats them both every chance he gets." Sugar Shack slapped his hand down on the bar and cracked up laughing.

A tall, chocolate vet bitch with finger waves came over to the bar. She stood on the other side of Sugar Shack ordering a vodka and cranberry. She wore a pair of tightly fitted leather pants. Her ass imprint in those pants stole every bit of Sugar Shack's attention. The woman glanced in the mirror behind the bartender and seen Sugar Shack's eye under the arrest of her ass. She craned her neck to the side to look his way. "Can I help you?"

"You can tell me if you taste as good as you look."

"If you want to find out the answer to that question then you going to have to dig deep into those pockets to get your answer."

"You ain't talking fruit to a squirrel baby. Let's say we blow this hotdog stand and go research that answer." The bartender sat her drink down. Sugar Shack pulled a fold of money then covered her glass with a five dollar bill and pushed it back to the bartender. She grabbed his hand to lead him out the door.

"Nice chatting with you players, but love calls my name."

Boss looked at the woman then back at Sugar Shack.

"Cookies and pussy huh?"

"Cookies and mothafuck'n pussy."

The woman lead Sugar Shack out the door.

Boss threw his attention back on Big Hunnid. "Big Hunnid, you ever heard the name Anthony Hack before?"

"Why that name sound familiar?" Big Hunnid thought about it for a second. "Yeah! I know who Boom is. Used to be a cold mothafucka with them bombs. Back in the day he was the man to go to if you wanted to make an example out of somebody by burning they whole block down, or making you small enough explosives to blow open a safe. Last time I seen that brother he was smoked out on Meth. He was so skinny, he could squeeze through the crack of a closed door and come out on the other side. A damn shame. Why you ask about him?"

"It was his burned body they found at my car that day."

"No shit?"

"Chief told me the dental records matched."

"The chief huh. I don't know why you and your mama keep that pig around."

"The chief's like family. Give me one legit reason why you don't like him?"

"I'll give you a few. Because he's the police,. I'm a black man in America and my uniform would always be orange before it ever would be blue."

Boss knew what Big Hunnid meant. He hated them boys in blue and rather go to jail than to ever be a friend of one. To Big Hunnid cops, no matter white or black, only existed to keep niggas in check for the greater good of the white and wealthy. Chief Aaron Hicks might've been cool with the family but Big Hunnid was still no fan of his.

"Man, Uncle Hunnid you just old and set in your ways. Not all cops are bad. Besides, he looks out for us when we find ourselves in a pinch."

"Yeah, at what cost? You might be right about not all cops being bad. But find one cop that would turn against his fellow brother in blue that is a bad cop. You'll be better off finding a unicorn. That's why I say all cops ain't shit. Chief Hicks is just king pig."

"Well king shit also told me Boom used to work for Rome. You know anything about that?"

"Rome used to use Boom back in the day to blow safes. Rome used to have his girls scout out rich tricks and hit their safes. Rome would give Boom the address and instructions to where the safes were. One girl would leave the back door unlocked for him while and keep the trick busy and away from the house. While Boom and another one of Rome's girls would hit the safe. They would bring all the valuables back and Rome would pay him."

"That's it? Boom never knocked anyone off for Rome?"

"Not to my knowledge. Scared a few people off but not kill them. Why you ask?"

"Because don't you find it strange that my father was killed in a boat explosion and Boom was a bomb expert that worked for his enemy. The enemy of mines and the same bomb expert that tried to off me. That's a lot more than a coincidence, Unc. Even Fleetwood sees that."

Big Hunnid's ears perked up. "What Fleetwood got to do with this?"

"He found out about Rome setting him up. After that, it didn't take much to get him to switch sides. He feeds me info on what Rome be planning and that kind of thing."

Big Hunnid's mind was running a thousand miles a second. "I don't doubt Rome's hand was what put both events in motion." Big Hunnid smashed his cigarette out in the ashtray. "Nephew, I told you from the get-go Rome wasn't someone you wanted to get in bed with. But you had to do it anyway. Now look at you, running around here damn near getting yourself blown up and locked up. You digging too deep into this shit, Boss. Let it go! Look at the fact you're still alive like a sign from God for you to leave all this alone, move out of state and move on with your life. It's only so far a man can dig until he finds himself stuck in the pits of hell trying to claw his way out."

"Can't you see? I'm already in hell!"

"If you believe that then you definitely need to put your shovel down. Believe me when I tell you, what's waiting at the bottom of this abyss will rip you apart first mind body then soul. This is bigger than Rome." Big Hunnid pulled out another cigarette and a book of matches from his jacket pocket.

"You referring to the Phantom."

In the middle of lighting his cigarette, Big Hunnid eyes glared up at Boss when he heard him mention the Phantom. "I know about him and Rome's ties."

"What do you know about the Phantom?" The cigarette moved up and down in the corner of his mouth as he talked. He squinted his eyes to block out the rising cigarette smoke as he shook the match extinguishing it's flame.

"I don't really know anything more than the stories I hear on the streets or on the news. The man's a ghost."

"A ghost that can't be touched. That should be enough to let you know the shit is too deep in the cesspool you'll have to swim through to get to him." Big Hunnid's phone vibrated on the bar. He was aware who was calling. It was a call he'd been expecting. He swiftly covered the screen with his hand as he picked it up before Boss could see the name that appeared on the screen. It was no way he was going to take the call in front of Boss.

"Everything alright, Unc?" Boss raised an eyebrow to Big Hunnid's suspicious behavior. He sensed he was hiding something.

"Yeah, I got some business I've got to go attend to. I'll catch you later, alright?"

"Sure."

Big Hunnid got up, tilted his hat to the side then gave Boss dap. He made his exit leaving Boss at the bar drowning in a pool of suspicion.

Big Hunnid jumped in his Cadillac DTS. His phone went off again. This time he answered. "Hello?...He ain't finna let this go. That boy is just as stubborn as Cadillac was. Now he's got Fleetwood on his team...You should've took care of Fleetwood when I told you to. I guess I got to do the shit myself. I'll call you when it's time to make the next move...Yup."

Big Hunnid ended the call. He wished Boss would've just took advice in the first place and not get wrapped up in that shit. Now it was too late and Big Hunnid had no choice but to clean up his mess. It's a cold world and shit was about to get a lot colder.

Chapter 14

Fleetwood was feeling top notch. Boss gave him back his three whores as a token of appreciation for trading sides. With the two white bitches he already had come up on, his original three back home made his stable five deep. All five of the girls were grinding their heels down to the soles making his money. He couldn't been happier. He could've stepped his new Giuseppe's in steaming hot pile of elephant shit and it still couldn't rain on his parade. It was as if the pimp gods were signing off on all his prayers, making his dreams come true.

He lounged back behind the wheel of his Cadillac, gangsta leaning to the side. His pinky stood erect while his right hand gripped the woodgrain steering wheel. He bobbed his head rhythmically up and down to Too $hort's song I'm A Player.

The big body Cadillac was going almost ninety miles per hour down Highway 94. He wasn't in any rush or anything. It's just when on the highway, the car floated like a ship at sea. And if you ain't paying attention you wouldn't realize how fast you were going. He shared a joint with Big Hunnid while they chopped it up. Fleetwood held the reefer smoke in his lungs as he smoke.

"Hear me pimp, I was balls deep in that pretty pink. Had her purring like a kitten with a mouse in her mouth. You dig?" He released the smoke through his nose while passing the joint to Big Hunnid. Big Hunnid placed his Fedora on his knee and took ahold of the joint.

"I ain't mad at you. I can't believe you caught her. That's the coldest snowflake I've seen this season. You got her cousin too? Knowing your kinky mind, you more than likely got them bitches to wrinkle sheets together." A guilty smile grew on Fleetwood's face.

"What can I say? I turned them into kissing cousins. Don't look at me like that. You know how I roll. It ain't no fun unless all my hoes bond."

Fleetwood swerved over to the far right lane to make the next exit. He slowed the big boat down to a cruise to blend with the speed of street traffic. His destination was to the Jazz In The Park Festival on the east side of town. The fun of jazz, dancing, laughter and women were festivities that would guarantee to enhance the good mood he was already under the spell of. Thoughts of knocking one of those excellent credit score having, lonely, white women there danced in his head.

Finding a good parking spot to park was more problematic than Fleetwood expected. He had to park four blocks away from the park, though the short walk brought no damper to his mood.

The great saxophonist Kenny G serenaded the crowd with the smooth sounds of the song Midnight Motion on his saxophone. The festival was flooded with white faces and a small sprinkle of ethnicity, just the way Fleetwood liked it. He felt more comfortable kicking it around a crowd of mostly Caucasian people, just as long as they weren't the hang a nigga for white power type. His philosophy was, being around his preferred crowd rather than a crowd of mostly blacks it was less likely to end in violence. But most of all he enjoyed being the rare species in the midst of curious white women.

Him and Big Hunnid made a maze through the crowd to the beer stand. "Say, my man, give us a couple of those

Coronas and drop a lime in them." Big Hunnid laid the beer vender a ten dollar bill on the counter. Him and Fleetwood toasted their bottles then turned them bottoms up.

Big Hunnid kept the cold beers flowing Fleetwood's way. After four more beers, Fleetwood was good and buzzed. Fleetwood saw it was the perfect time to pick his brain. He needed to know what all he knew. What all he could've revealed to Boss.

"I was just thinking the other day how smooth your boy Rome weaseled his way out of the challenge at the player's ball."

"You know Rome, he's always got a trick or two up his sleeve when it comes to staying planted on that throne."

"Let's be honest. We both know Boss was going to win it." Big Hunnid eyed his every reaction.

"I don't dispute that. Boss got a lot of game and I'm not adverse to him sitting on the throne."

"That's quite eccentric to hear coming from you. I didn't think the blood was warm between you and Boss, especially considering you being Rome's right hand." Big Hunnid was fishing for the words to fall out of the horse's mouth. He wanted to hear Fleetwood say he'd switch sides.

Fleetwood leaned closer to him so he could hear him. "Between you and me, me and Boss is good. But Rome—" He took a long swallow of his beer. "Fuck Rome. I've been his boy for -" He tried to count on his fingers and think back. "More years than I can remember right now. Never did that man wrong. Always had his back no matter what he was up against. But you know how that shysty mothafucka repaid me, Big Hunnid?"

Big Hunnid shook his head no.

"That nigga framed some work on me. Just so he could buy some time from Boss coming for him. Can you believe that shit?"

"You know you can't trust shit Rome does or says. He plays a cold game. He's so good at it. You can feel the icicles on your ass every time he talk."

"Amen to that." They toasted their bottles to that. "Oh but payback's a bitch if he can't pimp."

"What you mean by that?"

"What I mean is, he crossed me so I crossed him. I've been telling Boss everything he'd been planning and Boss been using that to stay steps ahead of him. He ain't waiting to next year to challenge Rome at the Player's Ball. He's coming for Rome at this upcoming Player's Picnic. With all the cops that's going to be patrolling the park, Rome won't be able to weasel his way out of the challenge this time. Boss is going to be king pimp and it ain't a damn thing Rome could do to stop it."

"What do you get out of all this, besides revenge?"

"For all my help, I got my hoes back for one. For another thing , Boss promised to keep me in the number two spot."

"You can't go wrong with a deal like that one." Big Hunnid put an arm on his shoulder. "Check it out though, you see that pretty thang over there in the white doctor's coat?"

Fleetwood's eyes followed the point of his finger to green eyed, strawberry blonde fifty feet away. She stood in line at a popcorn vender stealing glances at Big Hunnid from time to time. "She's been checking you out for the past five minutes."

"Is that right?"

"Um hm."

"Well, excuse me while I go run my magic."

"Handle your business baby."

Big Hunnid saw the shy face woman blush when Fleetwood walked smoothly over to her. It didn't seem to take much time or effort for Fleetwood to get her to digging in her purse and sneaking off to her car to stretch her womb out.

An hour later, Fleetwood returned to the park. He found Big Hunnid standing by a tree near the beer stand. "You wouldn't believe what just happened to me."

"Run me up the street to Pick'n Save real fast. I got to collect some money. You can tell me all about it along the way."

They sat in the parking lot of Pick'n Save. Sarah Smile, by Daryl Hall & John Oats sang on his radio. Fleetwood's mouth was running a million miles a minute with excitement about the doctor chick he just bagged. A tinted out black Chevy Malibu pulled up next to them. Fleetwood acknowledged the driver with a slight nod of his head.

"Big Hunnid, I tell you, I can die right now a happy man."

"It's funny you should say that."

Fleetwood looked over at Big Hunnid and his smile drained from his face. Big Hunnid had a 9mm with a silencer pointed at him. "Big Hunnid...What's going on? What's this about?"

"This is just business, nothing personal. I don't mean to throw out clichés, but nothing else seem to fit the moment. You was a hell of a player, Fleetwood. And a damn good friend. It's because of that I went out my way to be sure you had the perfect day. I wanted you to go out like a true player, Fleet."

"Why?"

"All I can tell you is you're disloyalty pressed the wrong person's buttons."

"Big Hunnid, we known each other since we were knee high to grasshoppers. You played at my house and I played at yours. Your mama spanked my ass and my mama spanked yours. You really think you could pull that trigger?" Fleetwood looked at him with pleading eyes that made Big Hunnid's heart pain. But it brought no change to his mission. He squeezed the trigger, hitting Fleetwood in the chest. Fleetwood's eyes widen with surprise. His hand touched the wound in his chest. He saw and felt the blood on his fingers with disbelief. He began to say something but was muted by another bullet Big Hunnid shot in the middle of his forehead. He fell face forward onto the steering wheel. Big Hunnid sat his body back up right. He placed Fleetwood's hat back on his head and straightened out his suit on his body. He made him appear as though he was resting instead of being dead. That way it would be hours if not days before someone notices him.

"There you go, player. I'll see you again when my time come. We'll ride that big Cadillac in the sky and have a good laugh about this." He wiped his fingerprints off the gun and left it next to Fleetwood's body.

Big Hunnid got out the car and hopped in the passenger side of the Malibu. He told the woman behind the wheel to drive. He dialed a number on his phone.

"It's done."

The caller on the other end was pleased. Though that didn't make Big Hunnid's tail wag. It just reminded him how deep he was sinking. Too deep to swim his way out. But it was the price he had to pay in the game.

Chapter 15

Isis browsed the business section of the downtown library. Dressed in jeans and a navy blue and gold Marquette Eagles basketball T-shirt, she blended in with the college campus students. Her finger traveled like a cursor across a line of accountant books then paused on volume one of the book The Art Of Money Getting; Or Golden Rules For Making Money, by P.T. Barnum.

Book in hand, she sat ducked off at a table next to a window in the far right corner of the library. Fifteen feet away at a table ahead of her were four young college girls. Two white, one Asian and one dark skin black girl who was talking like a valley girl to fit in with the rest. Isis envied them. Their lives were ideal. They didn't have to worry about the dangers of life or how to hustle their pretty little cashmere asses to survive. No, their only worries were finals and what party to go to next or should I call daddy for money or use my credit card?

They lived a life Isis had wanted for herself at one point in time. But as she thought on something Boss once told her, a smile crept onto her face. A square bitch ain't shit without a nine to five.

Times get hard, them bitches will fold like lawn chairs. True enough they'll graduate, go on in life, have successful careers and make lots of money. But them bitches still wouldn't be making more money than me.

She checks the time on her watch, 11:43 AM. So far the company she was expecting was thirteen minutes and counting behind schedule. She pulled up the text message to be sure of the time of their meeting. Her timing was accurate. Their tardiness was triggering her anxiety because they never been that late before.

Isis couldn't distract her mind with the book in her hand. Her worries were at an all-time high after what happened to Fleetwood. The Phantom was making examples. She didn't want to wind up a product of one of those examples. Boss's plan sounded solid but it only takes one thing to go wrong and she'd be the morgue's next customer.

A hand taps Isis on the shoulder. She twisted around. A man wearing Marquette Eagles hat was standing there holding a backpack. "Are you Isis?" His French accent was thick.

"Yes."

"I ran into your brother on the way in here. He was double parked and asked if I would give you this. He said you forgot your backpack in his car." He handed the backpack to Isis.

"Thank you." The man cut across a section of bookshelves and disappeared.

Isis unzipped the backpack just enough to peek inside. A sweatshirt was on top. She unzipped it some more to get her hand inside to move the shirt over. Her phone rang but she paid it no mind and continued to investigate the bag.

Underneath the shirt was bricks of heroin. It was the package she'd been waiting on. She shot a text to Boss. Right away, her phone started to ring again. She answered it on her way out of the library. "Yeah."

"That package touchdown to you?" Pimping Ball's voice came from the other end of the line.

"Yeah I got it. Why was the move made by proxy this time? Why weren't you and Tony Swag here like we normally do it? I don't like last minute changes in the plan. Especially changes I know nothing about."

"Chill out. The big man calls the shots and he's making us all move a little different these days. It's all about caution with him. You can understand that."

"To a certain extent. You make sure the Phantom understands it's my ass on the line if I get popped off with this shit because he want to keep me in the dark about what's going on."

"Bitch, just make sure you get the product to where it's supposed to go and collect that cheese. Or getting knocked by the police will be the very least of your worries." Pimping Ball left her hanging on the phone.

Isis was aware of the consequences he was talking about. Death and sometimes torture was the reward for any person who dared to cross the Phantom. Fucking with his money was a sure way to get put at the top of his hit list.

Isis started to walk out of Parnell's safehouse, on 91st in Silver Spring, after dropping off a couple of bricks. Feeling weighed down by the heavy stare of Parnell's eyes on her ass, she stopped at the threshold and spun around. "Parnell, did you lose your eyes in the crack of my ass? You sho' is looking."

"Dat mothafucka nice. I gon' lie. You need to quit playing and let a nigga tap that joint one good time. Umm hmm." Parnell bit his bottom lip as his eyes scanned her figure.

"You need to quit playing and come out them pockets."

"It's like that, huh?"

"You know it is. Stop acting like one of these broke niggas and pay for what you want." She tapped her hand on his pants pocket.

"Bitches throw pussy at me like rice at a wedding. What I look like paying for it?"

"Like a nigga that don't want to beat his dick or picture me while he fucks other girls when he could have the real thing. I mean…" She trailed a finger down his chest. "A real boss baller don't accept no substitutes for the real thing."

She was playing on his ego to get him to fall into her clutches. Isis was a pro at turning men into tricks.

"How much is it going to cost me to get that sweet ass of yours in my bed?"

"A grand."

"A thousand dollars!"

"You say that like it's a problem. I spend more than that on a night out at the club and I'm nowhere near balling like you." She turned around to give him closer view of her ass. "So if I can spare it on something as mini as that then I know you can spare it for your pleasure, baller."

Parnell stared down at her pretty, round rear and needed no further convincing.

"Locked that door and follow me to the back room." Isis closed the door but left it unlocked. She passed the front room then the dining room where two of Parnell's boys were planted at the table bagging up the heroin she just sold him. They arrived at the master bedroom. She tossed her backpack down bedside the bed.

"Hold on a second. I got to call Rome and let him know I'm good." Isis pretended to be speaking with Rome on the phone. While she was really talking in code to Boss's cousin Wayne. "Hey daddy."

"What's the business?"

"I'm on my way. I just wanted to tell you real fast about the show."

"What's the lay of the land?"

"It's going to be three judges at the competition banging their heavy gavels at us."

"Big guns huh. Ain't no sweat for me and my boys. We getting into position as we speak."

"Okay."

Parnell counted out a G and tossed it on the bed towards her. "Now let me see them cheeks in the air." She picked up the money and stored it in the backpack.

"Won't you prop open that window? It's going to get real hot in here."

Parnell used a small wooden pole to hold the window propped open.

"There you go. I got you a breeze flowing. Anything else?"

"A little music to start the show." Parnell smacked his lips on his way to the stereo sitting on top of the dresser.

"Aight, but don't expect me to start lighting candles and shit. I ain't trying to make love. I just want to fuck, get sucked and send you on your way."

The remixed song, Wet by YFN Lucci and Mulatto played low on the stereo.

"Turn it up."

Parnell obeyed her command turning it up a few notches. But it wasn't loud enough for her. She exhaled a loud breath and pushed him out the way.

"Move!" She spent the volume dial to the right, cranking the stereo up loud enough they could feel the vibration of the bass coming from the speakers. He tried to protest against the music being up so loud. Isis pushed his hands away from the knob and lead him back over to the bed. All his protesting came to a cease when she pushed down on to the bed and stripped him naked. She slowly took off her shirt, putting on a show for him. She danced on top of him. Still with her bottoms on she grinded her fat wet cat on his member.

"Ooh shittt! Baby, let me slip inside you." He took ahold of his member in his hand rubbing it against her camel toe.

"Not yet."

"Come on, girl. Just let me put the head in." Parnell set up on his elbows.

"In due time! Be patient, we'll get there. Right now just enjoy the show." Isis pushed him back down flat on the bed and continued her show.

Meanwhile, the front door of the house had crept open. In came Wayne, two Asian dudes name Vang and Lo, and

Wayne's main bitch, an Asian chick name Sushi. They could see hands moving across a table in the dining room. Wayne held up a leather glove finger to his lips. He signaled for them to move forward. Sushi got down low as she crept towards the dining room with her finger on the trigger of the Ozzie with the Wilson suppressor.

Sushi leaned against the wall outside of the dining room. She took sneak peek inside the room. One man sat at the head of the table weighing and bagging the heroin. A Draco was laid across his lap. The other man sat at the other end of the long rectangle shape table. He was blending several different powdered substances together with a wide blade and putting it into capsules. A Mac 11 laid on the table to the right of him.

Sushi looked back at Wayne and held up two fingers. Then pointed in front of and behind her, letting him know they were sitting at opposite ends of the table. Wayne turned to Lo, gave him the head gesture to go in.

Lo was 4' 9" with a seven foot attitude. Lo screwed the suppressor on to his two PP7's. He raised the gun up as he entered the room. The man caught a glimpse of Lo from the corner of his eye. Before he had time to react, Lo shot out one of the back legs of his chair causing him to fall backwards onto the floor. The second man reached for the Mac 11 but paused when he saw Wayne, Vang and Sushi rush in with their guns drawn.

His hand hovered over the Mac 11 as he debated in his head if he had enough time or not to grab it and lay a couple of them down before taking a few shots himself. Vang pointed his sawed off Mossberg right in the man's face.

"You do, you through. If you enjoy God's gift of breathing, then you better ease them hands back."

"Fuck you, you Jackie Chan looking mothafucka!" The man played tough but still eased his hand away.

"No, fuck you and suck my egg roll mothafucka!" Vang smashed the man on the side of the head with the stock of the shotgun. He fell out the chair on to the floor. He was knocked out cold.

"Vang, Lo, tie they ass up and load all the dope in the car. Sushi, you come with me."

Wayne and Sushi followed the sound of music to a room in the back. The door was closed. Sushi turned the knob as quietly as she could. She turned her head to Wayne and nodded. He nodded back at her. She pushed the door open and Wayne rushed in holding two customized pistols. A gold 9mm in one hand that had a brown handle and gold Louis Vuitton symbols on it. In his other hand was a chrome .45 with a pearl handle and silver Gucci on it.

At the sound of the doorknob slamming into the wall, Isis hopped off of Parnell. Parnell sat up wide eyed and was quickly losing his erection. "What the fuck is going on? And where you going?" Isis slipped her shirt on and grabbed her backpack. She blew him a kiss and hopped out the window leaving Wayne and his crew to handle things from there.

It was all a part of Boss's plan to stick it to Rome. Isis was to make the deliveries and Wayne and his crew was to steel them back and keep them for themselves. It was a plan that was sure to put Rome on the Phantom's murk list.

Chapter 16

Isis had four bricks left to deliver. The last four was going to a new customer that the Phantom added to the list. Another last minute change in the game plan that Isis wasn't too thrilled about.

She arrived at the meeting point. It was at the Pottawatomi Hotel. A casino hotel she was familiar with. She met johns there at least three times a week. She always felt safe there with all the security guards patrolling the hotel and cameras everywhere.

This time, she felt the complete opposite. Selling dope and selling pussy are two different things. Both came with consequences that were far from equal penalties. Prostituting could get her a ticket or a few days in jail. But getting caught with four kilos of heroin was a kiss goodbye to freedom. This time paranoia was setting in. She felt like the eyes in the sky were watching her and the security guards were following her.

She made a left when she got off the elevator on the third floor.

She knocked on the door of room 339. "Come in!" A woman's voice penetrated from the other side of the door.

For them not to come to the door and properly welcome her in stirred her nerves even more. She held a firm grip on her baby Desert Eagle that rested in the small of her back. Isis pulled it out and held it behind her in one hand and used her free hand to open the door.

Isis walked through clouds of smoke and the heavy skunk odor of weed filled the air inside the room. A woman stood in a wide stance in front of a small wastebasket with her back to Isis. From the gap between her legs, Isis could see the tobacco from a blunt she was busting open spill into the waste bin.

"I don't smell a deep dish, stuffed crust pizza, so I take it you're not my Uber Eats delivery driver with my food. That means you have to be Rome's delivery driver with my dog food. Either way I'm ready to eat."

Isis knew that voice. "Lulu?" Lulu, sprinkling weed into the blunt recognized twisted around and confirmed each other's presence. Isis slipped the baby Desert Eagle back into the small of her back.

"Hellll nahhh! What up, mami!" Lulu gave her a hug careful not to spill the weed out her blunt. "I should've known Rome would trust his bottom bitch to work for him on business he runs on the hush." Lulu had been out the game since Cherry died. She didn't know Isis had left Rome for Boss.

Isis started to tell her she no longer dealt with Rome like that anymore and that she with Boss. But she didn't want to explain why she was still hustling for him.

"Fuck all that, bitch. You hustling now?"

"Hell yeah. I wasn't trying to dance all my life. After that girl killed Cherry, I found my way out the game."

She sealed the blunt closed with her lips then dried it with a lighter. "Didn't nobody kill Cherry, that bitch overdosed."

"Ha! That's what everyone think. Have a seat." She pointed to the bed. Isis took a seat at the edge of it. "You my girl so I'm going to breakdown the real story for you."

Lulu put a flame to the blunt and brought to life. She took a couple of long puffs then passed it to Isis.

"What you think really happened?"

"I don't think. I know what happened. It went down like this. Cherry got out played by Queenie for her position as bottom bitch. Cherry was real sour about the shit. She used to come to work and vent to me about it all the time. What really put the hot sauce in her ass was when Boss asked Queenie to be his wife. That set her on fire. She said she was going to get rid of that bitch for good."

Isis dumped the blunt ashes in her hand. Lulu got an ashtray out the bathroom and gave it to her. Isis dumped the ashes out her hand and into the ashtray then dusted her hands off.

"So, what she do?"

"She asked if I knew anyone that could put that work in for her."

"You mean off Queenie?"

"Exactly. I told her to holla at Money Mike. He's the only one I know that could connect her with somebody that can get the job done and not tell."

Lulu reached for the blunt. "Did she do it?"

"Didn't that wedding get shot up?"

"But Cherry died before the wedding."

"Check this. Someone overheard her on the phone with the hitman plotting the hit. That's what sealed her fate. But Cherry had already paid half for the hit before she died. A third party paid the other half once it was done."

"Who is this third party person that paid the other half?"

"That I don't know. But what I do know is who took Cherry out and how."

Lulu's interest peeked even higher. She scooted closer to the edge of the bed.

"Who and how?"

"Okay listen, mami. My sister Marlena is a housekeeper, slash nanny, slash whatever domestic work position she could find worker. Well, she had got a job working as a nanny for this one woman's little boy. One day, the woman's sister comes over stressed out. They were in the front room talking and Marlena was listening at the top of the stairs. The woman kept going on and on about she had to do it. The lady she worked for asked what was she talking about. The woman then said, I killed her. She said she overheard her on the phone plotting to kill her so she killed her first."

"How did she kill her?"

"She said she switched her dope with a mixture of battery acid and heroin when she got in the shower."

"Oh shit! You serious?"

"Umm hmm. The kicker is guess who did it." She handed her the blunt.

"Who?"

"Queenie!" Isis put her hand over her mouth in shock.

"Yo, that's wild. I thought Cherry was your home girl. Why didn't you tell Boss this or get at Queenie yourself?"

"I mean, let's face it, Queenie was just defending her life. How I seen was I can get caught up in some bullshit Cherry brought on herself. Or I could use the situation to my advantage."

"How did that situation give you an advantage?"

"I needed to get rid of the road blocks in my way. I'm speaking of Los and Sugar. I wanted to take over the door game inside the clubs but they were in the way. I told Boss it was them that got Cherry hooked on that shit and it was a bad mixture they made that killed her. It was half the truth. I mean they did the same thing to Cherry that they did to me and many other girls. They started slipping heroin into her dope getting us hooked, turning us into junkies. They had to be stopped. Mission accomplished."

"But aren't you selling dope to them now?"

"Yeah, but I'm not tricking them into buying it or turning them out just to turn a profit."

"Make sense. Speaking of dope," Isis unzipped the backpack and tossed the two bricks of heroin on the bed. "You ready to take care of business?"

Lulu took the money out of one of the pillow cases and tossed to her.

"Always mami."

They made the exchange then said their goodbyes. When Isis open the door to leave, a man was standing there with food and drinks in his hand and his fist frozen in midair as if he was getting ready to knock on the door before it opened.

"Someone ordered a deep dish, stuffed crust pizza, with extra toppings and two liter Coke-Cola?" Isis had the munchies and that pizza was smelling good to her. She opened the box in his hand and took two slices. She looked back at Lulu.

"Thanks boo." She took a bite of one of the slices and left. She couldn't wait to put Boss on game about what she just found out. It was no doubt going to blow his mind just as much as it blew hers.

Chapter 17

An array of German and Italian engineered cars and other fancy vehicles lined the parking lot of Washington Park. The delicious smell of barbeque sizzling on the grill invaded the senses of anyone within a short distance of the park. A stereo system with eighteen inch subwoofers was plugged into a generator. It was playing full blast. Everyone was either drinking, playing dominoes, cards, eating or standing around talking. Some hoes were laughing and having a water balloon fight. It was the Annual Players Picnic.

Tony Swag and Pimping Ball were parked in Ball's Audi truck way on the other side of the park, away from prying eyes. The back door opened and Isis slid in. Tony Swag twisted around in his seat. "Took you long enough. You got the money?"

Isis through the backpack at him. "It's all here. If you got doubt enough to ask then won't you count it and see." She sat back in her seat crossing her arms. "Don't worry I'll wait."

Pimping Ball was ready to get to the festivities. Isis never came short before. From what he could tell by peeking inside the backpack Tony Swag was holding, it all looked to be there. He wasn't with wasting time counting the bread.

"Gone! Get the fuck out of here, you mutt bred ass bitch. If it's so much as one dollar short, I'll make sure Rome stomp the curve out your spine."

"Whatever." Isis rolled her eyes and climbed out the truck, slamming the door.

"Stop slamming my goddamn door! This a Audi bitch, not a Buick!"

"That hoe leave Rome and lose all home training. Call Rome and tell him that's a touchdown."

Pimping Ball dialed Rome using the hands free feature in the truck.

"Speak."

"That tramp just made the drop."

"Good. The Phantom's not making the pick up until later on tonight."

"Well, we going to keep the money locked in my truck until after the picnic."

"Nigga, have you gone mad? You ain't finna leave the Phantom's money lying around unattended. Absolutely not in this hood."

"You expect for us to babysit this cheese all day and miss the picnic?"

"That's part of what the Phantom pays you for. If you don't like it, it's always the option of quitting. We both know the consequences behind that." They heard the sound of people laughing and having a good time in the background of the call. "I got to go. Take care of that business."

Tony Swag slammed his fist on the center counsel. "Hey Mannn! I don't know what the hell wrong with you and that bitch beating up on my truck but y'all can stop taking y'all frustration out on my whip."

"My bad. This shit pissed me off. I've been waiting all summer for this damn picnic. I spent sixteen hundred dollars on this fit to show off at this event. Now we got to stay by the damn car babysitting the money. This some pure bullshit!"

Both back doors opened up. Pimping Ball and Tony Swag both startled, swiveled around in their seats to see who was getting in. Pimping Ball face frowned up. "Who the fuck is y'all?" Black bandannas covered Vang and Lo's face from the nose on down. They pointed their straps at Pimping Ball and Tony Swag's domes.

"Friends of Robin Hood, bitch. Now give us the money."

"Give you the money? What is you, like twelve years old, you little mothafucka?" Lo cocked back the slide on his gun then pressed it against the side of Tony Swag's head.

"Damn!" Tony Swag and Pimping Ball pulled out all the money they had in their pockets and handed it over to Vang and Lo.

"Thanks for the pocket change. While you at it you can hand over all that brick money too." Pimping Ball and Tony Swag exchanged looks of what the fuck.

"We don't know what you talking about player. We pimps, we don't partake in the economy of street pharmaceuticals." Vang didn't have the patience for their bullshit. He wanted to hit that lick as fast as possible so he could get his new Honda ready for racing that night. He took off his belt.

"What you undoing your belt for? Say bruh, I ain't with that funny shit."

Vang got the belt off then commenced to beating Pimping Ball in the face with the butt of his gun. Tony Swag, held tamed by the pistol pressed to his skull, begged him to stop. Pimping Ball swelled up quick.

Vang passed the bloody gun to Lo then took the belt and wrapped it around Pimping Ball's neck. Pimping Ball's face was leaking blood. He was gasping for air. He squirmed around in the driver's seat clawing at the belt around his neck. Vang pulled the belt so tight that his arms shook. "I'm not going to play games with you two. Give us the money or going to choke the life out of your friend then kill you too." Through gasping breaths, Pimping Ball ordered Tony Swag to give him the money.

Tony Swag was hesitant as he weighed his options. If that cheese wasn't available when the Phantom came to collect, him, Pimping Ball and Rome were all dead men. He was damned if he did and damned if he didn't. He made the only choice he believed he had.

"Here!" He gave Lo the backpack. "Now let him go!" Vang gave the belt one last hard tug then released him. Pimping went into a fit of coughs and heaving.

Vang slipped his belt back on as Lo called Sushi and told her to pull up. Within seconds, she was turning the corner and pulling up besides Pimping Ball's Audi truck. Vang and Lo hopped out the truck. With the backpack of money secured in hand, they slid into the ride with Sushi and sped off.

"Shit!! We fucked!" Now Pimping Ball was taking his frustration out on the truck by slamming his fist into the steering wheel. He pulled down the sun visor. "Looked what that bastard did to my pretty face." His blood boiled even hotter when he seen his badly swollen and bruised face. Blood leaked from a cut underneath his right eye. He was sure the bruises will turn into scars. He was even more certain he'd be a lot uglier in the morning.

"We have so much more to be worried about than your face. Rome finds out we ain't got that money, better yet, if The Phantom finds out we ain't got that money, we're dead." The fear and realization of what losing that money meant, was beginning to dawn on Pimping Ball.

"Why did you give them niggas the money!"

"Mothafucka you told me to! Anyways, if I didn't they was going to kill us both. I chose the best option for us."

"How's that, when we gon die anyway? Probably be tortured too."

"Because least now we have the chance to run, and a head start." Pimping Ball eyes begin to open to his logic. It wasn't no better option than the one Tony Swag chose.

"Then, we better get the hell out of here right now." He started the truck up and peeled out.

***

Wayne was incognito in a tinted out Subaru Outback. He spied on the festivities in the park from the library's parking lot across the street. Sushi shot him a text letting him know she picked up Vang and Lo.

Wayne was a busy man with all his clubs and various businesses. But gangsta shit like that was right up his alley. And for his favorite cousin , he was more than happy to lend his time and helping hand. For him and his crew to gain fifteen bricks of grade-A heroin in the midst was just icing on the cake.

He rang Boss phone and watched him pull the phone out and answer.

"Wayne, wassup?" Boss leaned against his Wraith, holding a bottle of MGD by the neck.

"Mission complete cuz."

"Everything go smooth?"

"Absolutely. My crew dropping that cheese off at your house now." He saw a wide smile appear on Boss's face.

"My nigga, that's what I'm talking about. You can free the hostages. I'll meet you back at my crib tonight." Wayne had kidnapped all the dealers he robbed to buy Boss some time. He didn't want Rome finding out they got hit, and put two and two together, until the day the Phantom was supposed to pick up the money. Because it was the perfect time to rob Pimping Ball and Tony Swag for the money. It would leave Rome no time to put together all the bread that was lost before the Phantom came to collect. Which in turn would be the nail in his coffin.

Chapter 18

Polo and Desmond walked across the park grass to where Boss relaxed on a picnic table nursing his beer. Boss was enjoying himself, chopping it up with Big Hunnid and Gator, another ol' skool pimp in the game.

Polo cleared his throat interrupting their conversation. Boss and the others turned around. "Polo, good to see you could make it." Boss put on a fictitious smile and embraced Polo to hide his feelings of distrust for him.

"Believe me, I wouldn't miss this for nothing in the world." He put his hand on Desmond's shoulder. "This my boy Desm-"

"Dez! You can call me Dez." Desmond never liked being called by his government name. His sisters had a habit of doing that. That same habit rubbed off on Polo. He wasn't about to have nobody making a habit of it.

"What's up with the bullhorn in your hand?" Gator asked Dez. Though Polo was the one to respond.

"Oh that's for me. Allow me to show you what it's for." Polo took the bullhorn from Dez then climbed on top of the picnic table. The bullhorn's siren went off. Everyone in the park, within earshot, attention fell on Polo. "Listen up, all you pimp, players and hoe slayers. I got something I want y'all all to bear witness to." He looked down at Boss. Boss seen Rome not far away fighting a smile from invading his face. Boss's stomach went into knots. He was getting a bad feeling in the pit of his gut. Something didn't feel right. "I hereby challenge Boss Bandz." The crowd went silent for a brief moment. All of a sudden they all bust out in laughter.

"What y'all laughing at?"

"Well, didn't you just crack a joke? If you ain't joking then you smoking nigga if you ever think you could win a challenge against me." Polo climbed down from on top of the table and stood face to face with Boss.

"Look in my eyes...Does it look like I'm playing with you. Either accept this challenge like a man, or back down and still look defeated in the eyes of everyone around here." The crowd found strong interest in the drama that was unfolding and gathered closer.

"You only have one bitch, Polo. I take that hoe and I put you out of business."

"A hoe don't make a pimp, remember? Speaking of putting someone out of business, I say we make things more interesting."

"How so?"

"Loser turns his back on the game and never returns." *Polo wasn't no real pimp. There was no legit way possible he could knock me for any of his bitches*, Boss thought to himself. But that look in his eyes was exuberantly confident which tightened the knots in Boss's stomach that much more.

"You know what, if you want to make a fool out of yourself, then why not? Let's give the people a little entertainment. I accept your challenge. Only if Rome agrees to stop running and accept my challenge today." Upon those very words, Rome's smile he'd been fighting back defeated his face.

"I accept." Rome quickly accepted. He had never replied so rapidly. It worried Boss. They were up to something. He knew it. He just couldn't quite put his finger on it.

Boss could've dismissed Polo's challenge as unworthy, just like Rome had got away with doing to him for so long. But a chance to take both father and son out the game all at once was food for his ego. Another moment in life to add to his reputation and legacy.

All Boss' hoes line up next to a tree. Everyone was there except Queenie. She was at the movies with Tweety. Kiwi stood feet away from them wearing a Gap shirt that showed off her belly piercing and some tightly fitted sweat shorts that displayed her fat camel toe.

Boss walked a circle around her with a look of displeasure. "I'm going to tell you what, you can keep this bitch. She ain't my type. Besides, I'm too picky to be digging in the trash for a bitch." It was a direct insult to Polo. He didn't know what Polo's gameplan was but he wanted to agitate him to knock him off point.

"Shoot yourself." It didn't work. Polo remained calm and proceeded to shoot his game at Boss's women. The first one he approached was Gemini. Boss had no worry about her going anywhere. He showed her the love she had always been missing in life. The love like she used to receive from her parents that she missed so dearly. Also, the love of a lover that made her feel like she was the only girl in the world. She wasn't going anywhere. She was stuck to him like gorilla glue.

Polo still tried and failed. He went down the line of women spitting game. Boss was taken back a bit by the amount of venom Polo now had in his game. His confidence was seemed limitless. If Boss hadn't known Polo for as long as he did, he would've sworn he had been pimping all his life. Rome had to have been training him.

Polo was down to the last two women in Boss's lineup. So far, his game hadn't convince any of the other women to change management. Though it still didn't dim the light of his confidence.

He went for Lilly, one of the renegades Boss knocked at the player's ball. Boss was uncertain about her. She had been acting real funny lately. He had to check her ass the other day. She had ran into some of her old friends from prep school when him and her were out and about. Boss had told her to come on and she ignored him and kept talking to her friends. She had forced his hand. She had displayed the two D's that a hoe never show a pimp, disrespect and disobedience. He smacked her to the ground then dragged her to the car by her long ponytail. The facial impressions that her friends displayed made her lower her head in embarrassment as they had pulled off.

"Check it hoe, you been mismanaged and taken advantage of. I say that because any hoe that ain't by my side must not know no better. If you got half a mind then you'd know I'm what's good for you. Switch up or stay stuck bitch." Lilly lifted her head then stood still as a statue. Though he didn't let it show, Boss was on pins and needles. He was starting to regret accepting the challenge. The realization of what was really at stake was beginning to set in. He didn't care if he lost the bitch. His worry was losing the challenge and being exiled from the game for good.

Lilly walked passed Polo and went over to stand next to Boss. Boss finally relaxed and exhaled the breath he had been holding. It was smooth sailing for him from there. The last girl left was Princess and he knew she wasn't going to choose him. She hated his guts for everything he put her through. He had shattered her into millions of pieces that only Boss had the skill to put back together. For that her loyalty was sealed with him.

Him and Polo locked eyes. Boss grinned at the disappointing look on Polo's face. Polo's eyebrows furrowed forming his face into a devilish look. He then directed his attention on Princess. He stared Boss down as he whispered in her ear. Boss was still grinning.

A moment later, his grin faded into a look of curiosity. Princess head was down but she was smiling. *Maybe she's just fighting back a fit of laughs at what he was telling her*, Boss thought to himself. Not knowing what Polo was saying in her ear couldn't defend that thought. It was a move Polo had stolen from him. A move Boss learned from the Holy Bible of Game. When a pimp whispers in a bitch ear during a challenge and gets her to react like Princess was doing by smiling, biting her lip and such things, he adds mystery and worry to a pimp whose woman is being macked on.

Polo stepped away from her and approached Boss. "I got to hand it to you, Boss. You got hell of game. You should be a warden the way you got these hoes on lock."

"Nothing but good game run through these veins."

"I heard that. Well, a deal is a deal. I guess it's time to say goodbye to the game."

"Don't worry, Polo. I'm sure you'll do just fine in any other field you choose."

"I can play well in any field. But I'm not the one exiting the game." Polo clapped his hands. "Bring that ass and that cash to daddy hoe." Boss' mouth went a gaped when he seen Princess go stand in front Polo. She went into her bra and presented him with a fat wad of bills.

"I choose you, Polo." Polo snatched the money from her hands then put his arm around her and Kiwi. The crowd was stunned by his defeat.

She crushed Boss's whole world then and there. Not in a million years would he have thought she would flip on him for Polo. He would've bet his life on that. In a way he did. His days in the game were over.

Rome came over cheesing hard and doing a two-step. "So long, Boss. It was a pleasure to watch you play. But it is an even more delight to see you retire." Rome was so excited that he stood up on the picnic table. "For you suckas that don't know, this here is MY boy! Y'all squares see how my, SON, took that nigga Boss out the game? That's right, the pimping in me is so strong I shoot the seeds of it!" Rome peered down at Polo with pride. "You did it, boy. You really did it. You accomplished what none of these other top notched pimps could. For that, I stand here the proudest father in the world at what you just achieved."

"I appreciate that, pops. I owe you a bit of gratitude for all you taught me." Rome smiled and fanned him off in a show of modesty. "Though I'm not done conquering." Polo climbed on top of the table and stood eye to eye with his father. "Now, I challenge you!" Rome chuckled then rested his hand on Polo's shoulder.

"Son, I know defeating Boss was thrilling for you. Maybe even got you riding the high of that rush right now but slow your roll." Rome brought his voice down to a tone that only could be heard between the two of them. "What the hell you think you doing! We had a plan. Challenging me wasn't a part of the script."

"Plans are like the weather, pops. They have the tendency to change at any given moment." Polo faced away to address the audience. "It is my mack given right as number two pimp to challenge the king at any given time, am I right?" The crowd agreed. "Then, tell me why is the king trying to deny me that right? Could it be he's too scared to except my challenge?" A mixture of boos and murmurs surfaced from the crowd. Rome needed to save face.

"You snot nose bastard. I taught you what you know. You think because you took out Boss you can move me off the throne? You're sadly mistaken. I will crush you like I would've crushed Boss."

"Keep it real, you couldn't crush Boss. If you could, you wouldn't have spent so much time dodging his challenges." Polo was pressing all the right buttons to get to him. Rome was fuming with anger. "But fuck all this talking. You saying in so many words I can't take you off that throne. Then, put some action behind that statement, gotdamn it!" Over a hundred pairs of eyes were locked on Rome awaiting his response. The pressure was on.

"I not only accept your challenge, I'll play it the same way Boss did. I won't even get at your bitches and still beat you."

"That's even better for me. The same consequences for the loser applies. When I win, you walk away from the game, for good. And vice versa." Rome made a ticking sound as he shook his head.

"Your life as a pimp is about to be short lived." He ordered his women to step forward. "Shoot your best shot, pimp."

"No need. I already did." Once again, he clapped his hands. "Peaches, come to daddy." Peaches came forward and presented him with a knot of money. "You should've known I had to have some kind of trick up my sleeve. I'm your son, and just as shysty as you."

Rome's heart fell into the pit of his stomach. Polo had outwitted him at his own game. He stood in disbelief right along with everyone else. Like Boss, he was finished.

Pimping Silky cut through the crowd. "Let's give a warm welcome to the crowned king of the game, King Polo." Slowly, the crowd went from a few claps to overwhelming applause. Polo smiled down on them as though they were the peasants of his kingdom.

Dez climbed up and stood next to him. Seeing all the people cheering for Polo was astounding to him. "That's a whole lot of love they showing you, big homie."

"Fuck them and their love. I just want the very thing that rules them, money and power," Polo said through clenched teeth and an artificial smile. Dez felt where Polo was coming from. To be good at ruling, he had to think like ruler. To be a ruler you have to be above your people. Therefore, you shouldn't be impressed by the things that impresses them. A ruler's main objective is to have control of that which he rules. Polo was seeking to do just that.

Having seen enough, Boss turned to leave. Sadness was riddled on the faces of his women. They too had to exit the game. Or explore the option of going renegade or choosing up to a new pimp. No longer being in the game, how far were they willing to follow Boss? The strength of their loyalty was soon to be weighed.

Chapter 19

Szzzzzzz! Szzzzzzz! Rome snorted two long lines of cocaine. It was so pure it made his nose run like faucet. He wiped it with his hand as he leaned back in his leather office chair with his head in the air.

His nerves were getting the best of him. He had made over eight calls to both Pimping Ball and Tony Swag. Neither of them had answered. He was trying his hardest not to imagine the worst case scenario, that they ran off with the loot. Throughout all the years they been making moves together, they never once crossed Rome or stole a dime from him. But the more time that passed without them getting in touch with him made them look more and more guilty to him of doing so.

Somehow, he had to get ahold of them. He was due to meet with the Phantom at 11:00 that night. The Phantom wasn't the kind of person that was acceptive to excuses. To him, excuses designed nooses around the neck of achievements, or around the nigga's neck that gives him one. If Rome didn't have his money, then he would be better off putting a bullet in his own head.

Half a million dollars may not seem like a lot of money to some, but it was a lot of money to come up within a matter of hours. A lot of money that Rome didn't have on hand. Enough money to get him and everybody close to him whacked.

Rome had a little money. But not enough to make up for the money he owed the Phantom, due to most of his bread being tied up in investments.

His phone rang, just as he was diving into another line. Instantly, he dropped the rolled up hundred dollar bill he was using to blow with. Quickly, his hand reached across his desk and snatched up his phone.

"Swag? Ball?"

"You crooked ass pimp. You set us up!"

"Who the hell is this?"

"Parnell!"

"What is you talking about I set you up?"

"You seriously going to play dumb with me? You sent that bitch Isis over to set me up. Them niggas kidnapped me and my boys and took all our work and money."

"I had nothing to do with that. Neither is your loss my problem!"

"It is now. You got until tomorrow to have my cheese. The whole sixty G's! Or I'm going to hunt you down and put more holes in you than a New York city street!"

"Take that hit up with—"

Click!

"Hello! Hello!" Rome looked at the phone screen and seen the call was no longer connected. "SHIT!" He smashed his fist into the wall puncturing a big hole into it.

He perched down in his desk chair resting his forehead in the palms of his hands. His head was weighed down by all the troubles that transpired that day. The people he allowed himself to trust were the same ones that stuck the knives in his back. It was one of the very reason he didn't trust people in the first place.

"Rome!" Hannah walked into the room with her iPad in hand. Her eyes darted straight to the football size hole he put in the wall. Her room was on the other side of it. She felt the vibration when he hit it.

"Bitch, what is it?"

"I was just checking on you. Is there anything I can do for you?" Her concern for him was heavy in her voice. It also was written all over her face.

"Unless you got a crystal ball that can tell me where I can find Pimping Ball and Tony Swag, get the fuck out!" He raked up four lines of powder and blew them.

"I don't have a crystal ball, but I can tell you where they're at." Rome looked up at her with eyes widened by hope.

"How?"

"You remember the purple iPhone I had?"

"What about it?"

"I sold it to Tammy last week." Tammy was Tony Swag's bottom bitch. Wherever Tony Swag had ran off to, you could rest assure she was sure to be.

"So." Hannah's thumbs went to work fiddling around with her iPad.

"So, all I have to do is go on here...and...use the Find My iPhone app to locate them...like so...Got em! I know this area and I know exactly where they at."

"Where are they?"

"Rome, your nose."

"What?" Blood started leaking out of Rome's nose from the purity of the cocaine. He was so transfixed on finding Pimping Ball and Tony Swag, he hadn't noticed it. She gave him a Kleenex from off his desk.

"They're at the Hide Away Motel right off South 27th Street."

Rome jumped to his feet. Expeditiously, he gathered his keys and things to leave out.

"Where's Ashley?"

"She's soaking and sobbing in the tub."

"Come ride with me. Bring your iPad so you can keep tracking them if they move." Rome rushed out the door with Hannah stumbling to stay in stride with him.

"You want me to go get Ashley?"

"No, forget her." Ashley was in her chest about being exiled from the game. It was nothing she loved more than the fame that came with being the king's whore. It was obvious to both Rome and Hannah that it would be only a matter of time before she jumped ship.

Rome's AMG was parked across the street from the motel parking lot. Tony Swag's bright red convertible Jaguar was parked next to Pimping Ball's Audi truck. The motel was small. No more than twenty rooms total. They couldn't tell exactly what room they were in. But they had it narrowed down to the four rooms which the cars were parked in front of. They couldn't go knocking on all four doors. Being that Pimping Ball and Tony Swag ran off with half a million dollars, they'd already be on point. If they were to spot Rome going door to door, they could easily escape out the back window or start shooting it out. Rome's best move was to have the upper hand by hitting them with the element of surprise.

"Go bust that move."

Hannah got out the car slipping her Gucci shades on. She walked across the street to the motel office. Peering inside, she seen a thuggish looking white boy in his early twenties manning the counter. He was sitting in a chair with his feet propped up on a table watching TV.

She situated her big titties in her bra so that they were on full display before going in.

The bell chimed when she opened the door. The man didn't take his eyes off the TV. They were glued on a Megan Thee Stallion and Cardi B video. "Gotdamn girl! Shake that big ole ass," he said while squeezing his crotch.

Hannah rolled her eyes. *Ding!* She slapped her hand on the bell on the counter.

"Rooms are forty bucks a night. If you want one, fill out the form on the counter," he said without taking his attention away from the TV.

Ding! Ding! Ding! Ding! Hannah rang the bell rapidly in attempt to get his undivided attention.

He jumped out of his seat. When he turned to snap out on the person for interrupting his video, he held his tongue when he seen Hannah. His eyes ran a lap all over her body and his whole attitude changed. He attempted to turn up his swagger by situating his hat on his head so that it was cocked to the left and untucked his fake silver chain for her to see.

Hannah looked down at his name tag. It really read Richard but a strip of electrical tape covered the last three letters.

"How can I help you, beautiful?"

"Hi!" Hannah was putting on her best ditzy white girl performance. "Whoa, that's a nice chain." Hannah touched the cannabis leaf charm on his chain.

"Oh, you like this? This old thang I paid ummm..." He pitched his eyes to the ceiling as if he was thinking. "A lil over twenty G's for it. You know, chump change."

"Really? And you work here?"

"Girl I'm about to own this place. Shoot, the only reason I'm working here is because my P.O. is forcing me to get a job. You know what I'm saying?" Rich was stunting hard. Trying his best to seem like the shit in her eyes. "Anyway, what brings a pretty lil thing like you to a dump like this?"

"I have a bit of a problem. I was wondering if you could...You know what, never mind." Hannah started to leave, Rich took ahold of her arm.

"Hold up, baby girl. Tell me what's good. Big Rich might be able to help you." Hannah was rolling her eyes in the inside. She hated people who referred to themselves as a third person. It was one of her top ten pet-peeves.

"My weed man stood me up and he couldn't have done it at a worse time. I have some of my sorority sisters coming in town tonight. I have been bragging about how the weed in Milwaukee was the best in the Midwest. They're going to be expecting to blaze out on some good and I can't find any. I was wondering if you might know where I can score an ounce of some real good weed?" Everyone in Milwaukee that smoked knew the Hide Away Motel always had good weed floating around. Rich chuckled.

"Girl, that's all you need is some green? You came to the right place. Your man Rich got you baby," he said patting both of his hands on his chest.

"Really? Oh Rich, you are a lifesaver. Thank you so much."

"It's nothing, girl. Do me a favor. Watch the door for me while I slip in the back and put that together for you."

"Okay, will do." Rich swaggered to the back of the motel office with his pants sagging.

Hannah was shaking her head. A grown man sagging his pants was another one of her pet-peeves.

Soon as Rich was out of eyesight, Hannah jetted behind the counter. She was in search of the check in form that could tell her which room they were in.

Rich was a bit of a slob. Office papers, candy wrappers and empty cans of Monster Energy drinks littered the desk. Ruffling through a scattered pile of papers, she found what she was searching for. A registry form with Tammy's name on it. The door to the back room opened. Rich was returning. Hannah confiscated the spare key to the room off the board and ran out the door before he could make it back to the front.

She was looking behind her making sure Rich wasn't behind her as she ran across the street and got back in the car with Rome.

"Where they at, Hannah?" Rome stared in the vicinity of Pimping Ball's and Tony Swag's vehicles.

"Room 13." She dropped the room key into his hand. Rome squeezed his hand tight around the red keychain that displayed the room number on it as he thought about what he was going to do to Pimping Ball and Tony Swag for trying to fuck him over.

"Go back in there and keep that front desk clerk occupied while I take care of this business."

"Oh God, daddy do I have to? He's such a douche bag. Can't I just wait here in the car?" The mug Rome shot her put her complaining to rest.

"I don't need that mothafucka calling the cops saying he seen shit. Ain't no cameras around here. But still, I need you to distract his ass so if shit get heated in there, and I have to lay them niggas down, he wouldn't have any information to give the cops."

Hannah went back inside the office. Rich jumped up from his seat in front of the TV when the door chimed. "Yo, where you go?"

"I heard you coming back to the front, I ran out to grab some blunts. " She held up a box of Swisher Sweet cigarillos. "I thought you and I could put one in the air. Got to make sure it's the best for my sorority sisters."

"Lock that door and let's do the damn thing then, girl." Hannah rolled her eyes and followed him to the back room.

Rome popped the trunk and grabbed the street sweeper. He crept over to room 13. With his ear to the door, he listened in on what was going on inside.

Pimping Ball paced the floor franticly with an icepack to his face. "Tony, we got to get out of here man! Rome's been blowing up our phones nonstop. It's only a matter of time before him or the Phantom come hunting us down."

"Ball, chill yo' ass out! I told you, we just waiting for my mans to come through and hit my hand for these jewels of mine he been trying to buy off me. After that, we in the wind. It takes money to lay low enough to be off the Phantom's radar." Tony Swag poured an assortment of diamond jewelry on to the bed out of a Crown Royal bag.

"Stop being greedy, Tony. Take that shit to the gotdamn pawnshop so we can get the hell out of here!"

"I'm not taking my jewelry to some damn pawnshop and have them assault me with some low ball offers. Nah, my mans is going to give me top dollar. You want to leave, by all means, do you. But I'm going to wait for my cheese."

Tammy was in the shower cleaning up from her last date. Pimping Ball and Tony Swag were too busy arguing. They didn't hear or see the door unlocking. What they did notice was the room start to grow brighter as sunlight poured in from the door starting to open.

Thinking it was a robbery, Tony Swag swiftly gathered his jewels. Pimping Ball chucked the icepack at the door and went for Tammy's .22 that sat on the mini fridge. He didn't even have time to point it at him before Rome was cocking the street sweeper in his face. Staring down the large barrel, Pimping Ball let the gun slowly fall to the floor.

"Where's the money!"

"We don't have it, Rome," Tony Swag explained with his hands in the air. Rome switched his aim onto Tony Swag.

"You better tell me where that money is and you better tell me now."

Tony Swag swallowed hard before spilling the details of all that happened.

"You dumb chumps let somebody rob you for the Phantom's money?"

"Look at my face. It was nothing we could do, Rome. They were about to kill us. At least this way we are alive to run."

"You were alive."

"Huh?" Just as Rome pulled the trigger splatting Tony Swag's head into thousands of pieces, Tammy came out the bathroom in a bathrobe and a towel wrapped around her head. As Rome turned the gun on her, Pimping Ball went for the .22.

BOOM!

A tennis ball size hole pierced through Tammy's chest sending her flying backwards.

POP! POP! POP!

Pimping Ball fired three shots at Rome, taking out a lamp and the TV and lodging the last shot in the wall. He attempted to squeeze off another round but a cartridge was jammed in the ejection slot. Rome walked up on him with the shotgun aimed at his head.

"Rome, wait a minute! Wait a minute! We can work this out! Tony got a hundred grand in jewelry in that Crown Royal bag. Just take that and, and, and give me a little time to hustle up the rest. Come on Rome, you ain't got to do this. We go way back, baby."

"You knew from the start that all our lives were on the line if anything was to ever happened to the Phantom's money. So if I got to die behind this shit, I'm going to take you mothafuckas with me."

BOOM!

"What was that?" Rich jumped up from his plastic chair in the back room of the office.

"What was what?"

"It sounded like gunshots. Did you hear it?" Hannah heard it. The loud blast of the shotgun couldn't be mistaken.

"No. You're high as shit. I think you're tripping. Turn up the music." Hannah went over to the radio and turned the music. Then, she pushed him back down in his chair and began giving him a lap dance.

"Damn baby, you know how to work that shit." Her distraction was working all too well as she felt him grow between the legs.

A text came to her phone. It was Rome. The message read: Get up out of there now. I'll be waiting around the corner for you...

She hopped off his lap. "Sorry Rich, I got to go. I got to go pick up my sorority sisters from the airport."

"Yo, yo, I get off in a few hours. Can I come kick it with y'all?"

"I tell you what. I'll run it by the girls and if it's cool with them I'll call you."

"Aight, cool."

Hannah left out the office and speed walked around the corner. Rome was parked in the middle of the block. She moved the Crown Royal bag with Tony Swag's jewelry in it off the seat and got in. Rome eased off into traffic, jumped on the highway and in minutes was far away from the scene.

Chapter 20

After much driving around and thinking, Boss pulled up in front of his house. Just as he did, Isis was headed out the house towards her car but changed directions when she seen Boss's car. She got in the passenger seat and close the door. She reached over and held Boss's hand that rested on the armrest. "You okay?" She asked him with genuine concern in her voice. She knew how much it meant to him to become king. She also knew it had to be killing even more to be exiled from the game.

"Where were you about to go?" Boss asked avoiding her desire to know where his head was at. Truth of the matter, his head was drowning in thoughts. He felt cheated not defeated but all and all he was still faced with one of his greatest fears, failure.

"I was gonna drive over to the apartments?"

"For what?"

"Remember we supposed to be working Miami this weekend. I was going over there to make sure the girls got everything together for the trip."

"You talking like I still got a leg in the game. Did you not just see me lose not only my position as number two in the game but I can't even play in the game. I'm finished, Isis!" Boss ended what he was saying by smashing his hand into the roof of the car causing Isis to jump a little. Feeling a headache coming on, he massaged his temple before seizing a bottle of Ibuprofen out of the center console. Four pills fell into the palm of his hand. He popped them in his mouth and washed them down with a swallow of Mountain Dew.

She wanted to say something but held her tongue. They sat in silence for fifteen seconds before she had a change of thoughts and told him just what she was thinking. "You know I can't believe you. You worked this hard just to become the number one loser."

"Bitch, what you say to me!" He snatched her by her shirt and cocked back his hand to smack her.

"Go ahead, hit me! It still won't solve your problem. Polo took you out the fold and now you going to let him fuck with your head to the point you trying to beat your bitch for trying to get your mind right? All I was trying to say daddy was ever since I've known you, you have never been a quitter. So don't start now." Boss relaxed his hand and let go of her shirt then melted back into his seat.

"You say that like I have much of a choice to stay in the game or not."

"You do! True, you could never be recognized any longer amongst the elite but can't nobody stop you from pimping."

"Do you hear yourself? What do you think I got in this game for, to be recognized as the king of it all."

"And here I thought you got in the game for the money. Since when have you ever needed any nigga's recognition for your pimping? Your whores know you the greatest and that's why we with you."

"Yeah but for how long? Knowing I can't be recognized in the game any longer, how many of them bitches you think are going to continue to stick around? You know as well as I do, most of them hoes are going to split like a gymnast."

"Don't say that. You got some down ass bitches on your team that's going to ride with you regardless." Her attempt to keep him in good spirits was failing. His wounds were too fresh to be healed.

"Give up the optimistic speech. You know damn well I'm preaching the gospel to you. That's why you was really going over to the apartments. You wanted to try and stop them from leaving. You can't stop them from running. That's just what fame riding ass hoes do. Remember, it wasn't that long ago you were busting that same move. You had concrete feet in the game when Rome was the king. But when you saw he was pushing you to the back of the line and I was climbing to the top about to bring his reign to an end, you jumped on my bandwagon. Hell, I'm sure it won't be long before you'll be popping that pussy for Polo."

Isis could see he was only lashing out to try and push her away. His feeling of failure was causing him to self-destruct and he didn't want her to drown in his misery. She knew that but knowing that didn't stop the sharp dagger of his words from piercing her heart.

"You think I'm with you just because of the fame. If that was the case, I would not still be here by your side. I wouldn't be putting up with helping you care for your wife who couldn't stand me and I couldn't stand her when she wasn't disabled. I would've been took her ass to the top of Peekaboo Hill and pushed her wheelchair down Center Street and let her get hit by a car speeding down 3rd Street. I'm with you because I love you. You can say Isis I don't want you hoing anymore, I want you to get a job at McDonald's and I will be there flipping burgers to get yo money because I love you enough to follow to the ends of the earth. You not knowing what you got is what's making you a loser." Isis got out of the car slamming the door behind her.

***

It was ten minutes to nine. Time was of the essence and Rome was no closer to having the Phantom's cash. But at least now he knew where it was and just how he was going to get it back.

Switching out of his AMG and into Hannah's 2016 X1 XDrive BMW truck, Rome sat on the passenger side and watched a woman stuffing bags of clothes and other things into the trunk of her car.

"What you want me to do, daddy?"

Rome reached into the glove department and took out a bottle of Chloroform and a face towel.

"Just keep the car running and ready to burn out of here as soon as I'm back in it," he said as he poured the Chloroform on the towel. Getting out of the car, he opened the back door then did a quick 360 look around to be sure no one was watching.

Her sweatpants sagged a little, exposing the top of her orange satin thong. The woman was working up a sweat stuffing bags of clothes and other things into the trunk. She was oblivious to what was about to occur. She didn't hear him coming as he silently crept up behind her. He held his breath as he got closer to her trying to keep his silence. He knew she was a real feisty woman and if she heard him, she would put up one hell of a fight and Rome wanted to avoid making a scene.

He was only a few steps away from her when his foot crunched down on a twig on the ground. The sound of the twig cracking in half made its way to her ears. She spun around but it was too late. Rome rushed over to her, forcing the Chloroform rag over her mouth muffling her screams. She fought hard scratching at his face but her battle lasted only a few seconds before the Chloroform took effect and she fell limp in his arms.

Rome scooped her up and carried her to the car. He put her in the backseat and got in. He couldn't even slam the door close good enough before Hannah had the truck in drive and was smashing out of there.

"Slow this mothafucka down, Hannah! We don't need no extra attention our way."

Hannah slowed the truck down to a legal speed then sparked a cigarette to calm her nerves. She's always been down for whatever but she never had to do nothing more than sell pussy to prove that. Now, she was assisting Rome in murder and kidnapping. It gave her an adrenaline rush and she loved it.

Rome reached and snatched the cigarette out her mouth and tossed it out the window before she could take another pull of it. "What I tell you about smoking that poison around me."

"I'm sorry. Where am I going?"

"Just keep driving. I'll tell you in a minute." Rome pulled his phone out and called Boss. He picked up on the fourth ring.

"Yeah," Boss answered in a low groggy tone.

"Did I wake you, pimp."

"What do you want Rome?"

"I want the money and dope back that you stole from me!"

"You can kiss my ass on that. You ain't got shit coming. You know I stole the shit at first to get you to give up your position as number one. But now, neither one of us have a foot in the game. So, I think I would do better by keeping the shit."

"I don't think so. You know who shit you stole?"

"I don't give a fuck about the Phantom. Don't let this pretty boy shit fool you. I can come out this suit and throw on a hoodie and we can spark these streets up like the Fourth of July. You feel me?"

"I'm not trying to hear all that tough talk. It's a lot more on the line than yo' young, dumb ass know." Rome laughed. "I got that mother of yours laid across my lap and I'm caressing her head with the barrel of my 357 right as we speak."

"What! Rome, you hurt or lay a hand on my mother, I'LL KILL YOU!"

"Then, listen up mothafucka, because I'm going to put it to you like this, if you don't have yo yellow ass at the Ambassador Hotel by ten o'clock with all my money and dope you will never see this bitch alive again. You so much as a minute late or dollar short and she's done breathing. YOU GOT THAT?"

"I'll be there with yo shit."

"Good." Rome disconnected the call.

Hannah looked over at Rome. "So, we're headed to the Ambassador?"

"Nah, we're going to the airport. We got somebody to pick up before lil miss feisty wakes up."

Hannah checked her side view mirror before changing lanes and hoping on I-41 headed to the airport. Rome looked down at a sleeping Tweety. She still was just as beautiful as she was when he had first met her. Lying in his lap like she was, reminded him of how she used to willingly do that very same thing when they would lay up after she finished making her quarter for the night. Deep down, he missed the feel of her. Those satin walls of hers that squeezed his dick so tight was never a forgotten thought in his mind. Just the thought of it and the smell of her made his dick hard. He chuckled to himself at how she still had that effect on him. There had yet to be another woman that could compare to her on any level. She was his perfect woman until she became his perfect enemy. Remembering her betrayal made his face frown up and dick go soft. He sat back in his seat and stared out the window putting his train of thought back on the mission at hand.

Hannah was sneaking peeks at him in her rearview mirror. She could see the worry in his eyes and knew they were in some deep shit and prison or their untimely death was sure to be the outcome. But hell or jail she was riding with him to the end.

Chapter 21

"Bitch, don't let that shit spill on my carpet!" Polo yelled then grinned at the site of Kiwi trying to lick the Ace Of Spades that fizzled down the side of the champagne flute before it hit the floor.

The kitchen and front room of Polo's three bedroom townhouse was crowded with people celebrating his victory. Everyone was laughing and having a good time, everyone but Princess.

Polo glanced over at her. By her demeanor, it was evident she wasn't in the spirit of celebration. Princess sat in a sofa chair in the corner of the front room with her elbow perched on the armrest and her head resting on her fist. Her left leg was crossed over her right one that bounced up and down. She stared down at the floor with a look of anger.

Polo excused himself from the presence of one of his guests he was speaking with. He grabbed a glass of champagne from a serving tray a woman held up and smoothly walked over to Princess. He kneeled down on the left side of her. He held out the champagne glass for her to take. She didn't even bother to look in his direction. Polo looked around the room with a fake smile plastered on his face. He gave a few head nods of greeting to some guests that had just arrived then turned his attention back to Princess. Swiftly, he took ahold of the back of her neck with a grip that made her feel like a mouse caught in the embrace of a boa constrictor.

"Bitch take this glass," he told her through clenched teeth. "That funky ass attitude of yours is beginning to stink up the place. Take this damn glass and fix it!" He pushed her away so hard just before releasing his grip that her head bounced off the headrest of the chair.

Princess scowled at him as he stood up and walked off with that same imitation politician smile on his face for his guests.

It hadn't even been a whole day she's been with Polo and she was already feeling like a prisoner. So badly did she want to call Boss to come get her so she could explain to him her reasoning behind her choosing Polo. But she couldn't find the words that would make him understand her logic.

Plus, Polo was keeping a close eye on her. She tried to use her phone earlier and he was on her ass in seconds to see what she was doing or who she was communicating with. When he looked at the phone and seen it was Boss's number she was attempting to text, he backhanded her across the face and took it leaving her with no way to communicate with anyone without his permission.

Across the room, Peaches had a devilish smile on her face. It made her feel warm and tingly inside seeing Polo handling Princess rough. It wasn't a sexual feeling she was feeling but a feeling of excitement from seeing her competition falling out of grace with her prize.

Peaches walked over to Polo with a bottle of champagne to fill his glass. She rested her hand on his back as she filled his glass. She got so distracted looking over at Princess with an evil smile she didn't see the glass was starting to overflow.

"BITCH! Watch what the fuck you doing. These are Christian Louie's! Get yo punk ass down there and clean that shit off my shoes," Polo said while throwing a handkerchief in Peaches face.

The whole room laughed at her while she got on her knees and cleaned his shoes. She looked over at Princess and seen she was now giving her a devilish smile. Princess mouthed the words *Karma's a bitch*. Peaches quickly finished wiping off his shoes then stormed out of the room giving Princess a good laugh.

Most of the guests Polo had over were thugs, barbers from his old job, some pimps and their whores. Nobody Princess socialized with was in attendance. Not only did she feel out of place, she had no one to lean on to use their phone. She needed to contact Boss immediately. He had to know what was going on even if she couldn't find the words to make him understand she was going to damn sure try. It was more than her heart and feelings on the line, she had to find a way to contact him before it's too late.

The doorbell rang making Kiwi pop up like a pop tart jumping out a toaster to get the door. It just so happened, like her prayer to God being answered Princess recognized the next guest that came through door. A brief smile of hope appeared on her face. She didn't want to seem too excited in case Polo was watching her reaction.

Netty, a thirty-six year old vet chick Princess used to dance with back in St. Louis walked through the door. Netty had a redbone complexion. Her honey colored eyes, long Indian like hair and big titties drew attention everywhere she went. People would think her and Princess were sisters whenever they were together.

Netty came in following behind her pimp, Pimping Debonair. It didn't take long before she noticed Princess over in the corner. Her eyes got big when she saw her and she wanted to scream with excitement from not seeing her homegirl in so long but Princess quickly put a finger to her lips giving her the shhh sign. Netty killed her excitement and calmly walked over and took a seat on the arm of the chair.

"Hey girl!" She reached over to hug her but Princess pushed her back while checking to see if Polo was watching. He wasn't. He was deep in conversation with one of his boys. "Damn what's up with the cold shoulder?" Netty gave her a look of confusion.

"It's not like you think, Netty. I ain't trying to be cold to you. I just can't let this nigga find out that we know each other."

"Who?"

"Polo!"

"Why?" Princess looked her dead in the eyes while she broke everything down to her. "Damn that's some fucked up shit he did. So, what you going to do?"

"I got to get ahold to Boss."

"Hit him up!"

"I can't! Polo took my phone."

"Here, take mines." Netty reached for her phone in her bra. Princess stopped her.

"No, he's been watching me like a hawk. He sees me get that phone from you and that's my ass."

"Well, this is what I'm going to do. I'll go to the bathroom and hide it in there. You just go in acting like you using the bathroom."

Princess's eyes brightened at the idea. "That's a good idea. Put it inside the dirty clothes hamper."

"Say less, I got you." Netty got up casually working her way through the room sparking up conversation with other guests so Polo wouldn't get suspicious about her conversing with Princess. She wanted it to look as if she was just working the room and getting to know everyone in attendance.

Once she felt she put on enough of a show, she made tracks to the bathroom. A couple of minutes flashed by and she came walking out the bathroom. She winked her eye at Princess then took post next to Pimping Debonair.

Princess got up trying not to speed walk to the bathroom but she couldn't slow down the urgency of the situation had her nerves going. She couldn't even get in the hallway that lead to the bathroom get enough before Polo had cut her off.

"Where you think you're going?"

"I'm going to the bathroom. I got to pee!" Polo searched her eyes for a moment making her feel uneasy.

"Alright, I'm coming with you."

"You gonna stand in the bathroom with me while I use it? Really? You already got my phone. We're on the fourth floor I can't go climbing out of the window."

"Rest yo mouth and relax. I'm just going to stand outside the door." He held out his hand motioning her to continuing walking. Princess rolled her eyes and continued making tracks to the bathroom. Her hand gripped the doorknob and twisted the door open but Polo pushed her out the way, cutting in front of her.

"I'll go first," he said closing the door behind him. He didn't have to use the toilet. He was just checking the bathroom before letting her in there. Princess was aware of his intentions. She stood on pins and needles as she heard him rambling through the bathroom. She was hoping he didn't find the phone in the laundry basket during his search.

When he exited the bathroom, Princess's heart was racing fast. The look on his face as he stood at threshold of the bathroom door made her think he found something wrong. But her worries were subsided when he spoke his next words.

"Gon in there. Hurry up too. I got to get back to my party."

Princess started to walk past him. He cut in front of her once again. This time lifting her chin up and kissing her on the mouth.

"You just watch, I'm going to make you ass love me again." He stared deep into her eyes giving all sincerity to his words.

"I got to pee." Princess gently removed his hand and walked into the bathroom closing the door behind her. Soon as she was safely inside, she quietly turned the lock on the door and turned on the water so Polo wouldn't hear what was going on in there. Then, she went straight for the laundry hamper. It was filled with dirty clothes. Working as fast and silently as she could she managed to empty out the entire hamper and found nothing in the pile of funky clothes. Her mind was like a pinball machine bouncing off different scenarios of what went wrong. Did Polo find the phone and not say anything yet? Why would he do that, to catch me in the act of searching for the phone? Did Netty lie to her? Did she tell Pimping Debonair what my situation in hopes of getting on their team and instead Pimping Debonair ratted me out to Polo? Her mind was all over the place.

Whatever the situation was, she didn't have much time to waste on thinking about what might've happened. She had to put everything back before Polo started to wonder what was taking her so long in there.

Grabbing her last handful of clothes to put back in the hamper, she felt something vibrating. She quickly dropped the pile of clothes and began searching through them then. BINGO! Inside a pair of brown Mike Amiri jeans, she found what she was looking for. Netty had come through after all and knew exactly how to hide so Polo or no one else would find it.

Princess took a seat on the edge of the tub. Her fingers went to work frantically dialing Boss's number. "Come on Boss, pick up." Her right leg bounced up and down as she waited nervously for Boss to pick up the phone.

The phone rang and rang then went to voicemail. Princess hung up and called right back. Again, the phone rang and rang with no answer.

Polo rapped hard at the door making Princess jump. "What's taking you so long in there!"

"Damn, it's hard to when you standing at the door. I'll be out in a minute."

"You got sixty seconds before I come in there." There wasn't enough time for Princess to keep blowing up Boss's phone so she began typing him out a text.

"Times up! Get yo ass out here, Princess."

She wasn't finished with the text yet. "Give me a minute, I'll be out there."

"What the hell is you doing in there?" He said taking hold of the doorknob. He attempting to open the door. "Bitch, what the fuck is this door doing locked? Open it up now!" Her thumbs moved like tiny jackhammers on the phone. She was determined to get her message out to Boss.

Dez noticed Polo wrestling with the bathroom doorknob and approached him. "What's good big bro, everything aight?"

"Fuck nah, this bitch up to something. She locked the door."

"You want me to bust the door down?"

"Nah, I don't want to make a scene in front of the guests. I don't want mothafuckas thinking I can't handle my own household. Go get the key out of the top drawer in my bedroom."

Dez hurried off to the bedroom and came back with a ring of keys, holding four keys on it. Polo was fumbling with the keys trying to find the right one. Princess had finished her text just as she heard a key slide in the door. She attempted to send it but there was no signal.

"Shit!" She stood up walking around the bathroom in search of a signal. "Come on baby, give me just one bar."

Another key slid in the door. She stood on the toilet. Still no bars. She had to hurry. It wouldn't be long before Polo found the right key. She didn't care what he did to her, all she cared about was Boss getting that message. She stood on the sink, nothing. Another key slid in the door. She got off the sink and went and stood in the shower. She walked around the tub then opened the window and held the phone out of it. She shifted her hand a little to the right and caught three bars.

"YES!" She sent the message.

Polo slid the last key in. When he opened the door, the toilet was flushing and Princess was standing at the sink washing her hands. Polo's eyebrows were furrowed and his chest was pumping up and down. "Damn, what you come barging in here for?"

"Bitch, come here!" Polo snatched her by the arm and began searching her then searching the bathroom. He found nothing.

"You find what you was looking for?"

Polo mugged her hard. "Get yo ass out of here and back in the living room," he said pushing her out of the bathroom.

Princess felt more at ease now that she got her message out to Boss. She only hoped that he would read it in time.

Chapter 22

Boss laid in bed with his back against the headboard, rubbing Queenie's big belly while she slept. She was damn near ready to pop.

Out the corner of his eye, he could see the light from his iPhone screen glowing. A quick peep at the screen showed he had a text message from a number with a St. Louis area code. He exhaled a breath of frustration and ignored it.

He had been getting calls since he got home from different pimps saying they just knocked one of his hoes. Quickly, hoe by hoe his stable was being dismantled. It was killing him in the inside. The only ones he had left was Isis, Macita, Gemini and Sapphire.

After getting the call from Rome, he couldn't bear to hear any more bad news. He turned his phone on silent while he thought a moment about how to handle the transaction with Rome. Even though it was his mama's life was on the line, he still had to stay in the mind frame of a pimp. The Holy Bible of Game said, Every situation dealing with a pimp is a pimp situation and should be handled with ice on his emotions to keep his cool and a calm mind to keep good game on his tongue.

He planted kisses on Queenie's lips to awaken her. "Get up baby, we got somewhere we got to be."

"We go to beach?"

"No, we don't go to the beach baby. I got to take care of some business," he told her as he began dressing her. He picked up his keys and phone. Looking at the time on his phone, it was 9:39 PM. That gave him twenty-one minutes to make it from his house on Lake Drive to the Ambassador Hotel on Wisconsin Street. Driving Queenie's Bentley GT coupe with V-12 engine, made twenty-one minutes more than enough time for him to get there.

He took the phone off silent, slipped it into his pocket and left out the door with Queenie and Lil Boss.

They made it to the Ambassador Hotel with eight minutes to spare. Boss got out the car and came over to the passenger side to get Queenie and Lil Boss out of the car. Seconds later, Big Hunnid pulled up in front of his car with Wayne and got out. Boss called him and let him know what was going down. Big Hunnid was the only one he trusted right then to keep an eye on Queenie while he handled business with Rome.

Big Hunnid walked over, leaned against the car and lit up a cigarette. "I appreciate you watching after Queenie and Lil Boss while I take care of this."

Big Hunnid exhaled a cloud of smoke before responding. "What is family for if we can't come to each other in our time of need. Listen, you be careful in there and make sure you get that sister of mine back safely. We'll deal with Rome another time."

"You better believe that." Boss passed Lil Boss to Big Hunnid. "Stay close by.

"I'm going to take them to Michael's up the block to put something in their stomachs."

"Cool, I'll hit yo line when it's all done." Boss gave Queenie a kiss on the lips. "Go with Big Hunnid, baby, I'll be back shortly."

Big Hunnid took her by the hand and walked them to his car. Wayne scrolled over to Boss.

"You ready cuz?" Boss retrieved two Glock 40's from his glove department, cocked them back then slid them into the small of his back and picked up the bag of money.

"Let's roll."

Inside the hotel lobby their shoes echoed off the marble floors but became silent when they reached the red carpet that lead to the elevators.

Boss' phone rang. "Hello."

"You cutting it close, ain't you?"

Boss checked the time, 9:57 PM.

"I'm here, what's the room number?"

"Room 303."

Wayne pressed the button for the elevator and handed over the dope to Boss. A moment later, the golden elevator doors slid open and they took it to the third floor. Wayne went to the room directly next door to the right of room 303. He tapped on the door. A man with a towel wrapped around his thin waist came to the door.

"Can I help you?" He asked breathlessly with sweat running down his face.

"I'm sorry to disturb you sir and this may sound a bit awkward of a request, but you mind if I come in and hang out for a minute?" The man looked Wayne up and down.

"Are you some type of lunatic or something! Hell no!" He tried to close the door but Wayne stopped it with his foot.

"What in the world is going on?" A naked, middle aged white woman came up behind the man behind the door.

"Helen, call the front desk and tell them it's a stranger at our door trying to get in."

"What does he want?"

"This lunatic wants to come in and hangout with us." Helen checked Wayne out, letting her eyes lock on the bulge in his pants.

"I don't see nothing wrong with a little company, Carl. Come on in, mister?"

"Long John," Wayne said and she smiled pushing Carl out the way and letting Wayne inside. Wayne pointed to his ears then at Boss letting him know he was on point and will be listening in through the walls.

Boss knocked on the door. Hannah swung the door open and gestured for Boss to come in and take a seat. "Where's my mother?"

"That's question for Rome not me."

"Then, where's Rome?"

"He'll be here. Is that his shit?" Hannah asked reaching for the Nike bags in Boss's hand. Boss snatched the bags out of her reach.

"He'll get this when I get my mama."

Right then, the bathroom popped open. In one swift motion, Boss dropped the bags and pulled out his Glocks from the small of his back aiming one of them at Hannah and the other directly at the bathroom.

Rome stepped out of the bathroom drying his hands with one of the hotel towels. "Easy on those triggers pimp before an accident happen."

"If I squeeze these triggers, you can be guaranteed it won't be an accident, pimp. Now where's my mama?"

"Chill, she's close by and safe. Before we get into all that, I think it's about time you and I have ourselves a little talk."

"We ain't got shit to talk about. I got your shit right here. Now go get my mother."

"Believe me, what I got to say is worth hearing. It's going to change your whole world." Rome swaggered into the main room tossing the towel on the table then gesturing for Boss to take a seat with him. Boss thought for a moment. What could Rome have to tell him? Is it some kind of game he was playing to buy time to carry out a plot against him? Boss didn't know but his curiosity was getting the best of him.

"Nah, I rather stand. But she can sit."

Rome nodded his head and she came over and sat down next to Rome.

"Have it your way. I know you're probably wondering why is the King of the pimp game -"

"Ex king!" Boss corrected him.

145

"Ex King, of the pimp game moving dope for the Phantom?"

"That ain't hard to put together. Yo game ain't shit and you a sucka for love ass nigga whose better off having your whores sell dope for you than their own asses. My mama already told me about how she chose my pops over you and the sucka attack you had behind it. Yeah, she's my mother but still you killed your own best friend over a bitch? How low down can you be?"

"Despite how you may feel about me Boss, you couldn't be further from the truth."

"Then, tell me what the truth is and spare me the lies."

Rome picked up a bottle of Louis 13 and poured up two double shots. He slid one glass across the table for Boss to have. Boss slid one of the guns back in the small of his back reached over and took possession of the glass. Eyes deadlocked on Rome and Hannah, he leaned against the wall and drained half the contents in the glass in one gulp. Then, he waved the gun at Rome to keep talking. Rome leaned back in his chair with stippled fingers still portraying the arrogant aura of a king.

"It's true me and yo father had beef over your mama. But what you and everyone else don't know is that me and Cadillac had squashed that beef and our bond became thicker than a Mississippi hooker."

Boss pushed off the wall. "That's bullshit!"

"You gon talk or listen?"

Boss pursed his lips and leaned back against the wall. Rome tried to continue but a knock at the door interrupted him. Boss sat the glass on the table and slid his other Glock back out aiming it at the door.

"You expecting company?" Boss said sarcastically while pointing his gun at Rome's dome.

"Actually I am. That will be your mama and someone else that I believe could explain things to you a little better than I can."

"Who?"

"How about I show you." Rome got up slowly and walked over to the door. Boss's grip got tighter around the pistol grip as he anticipated who might come through the door.

The door creaked opened and in walked Tweety. His hand relaxed on the trigger and he went over and held her tight in his arms. "You okay? They didn't hurt you did they?" He said look her over.

"I'm fine baby." The presence of another figure coming through the door was felt by Boss drawing his attention in that direction. When he laid his eyes on the figure coming in, he thought he was hallucinating. The man stepped towards Boss and was now face to face with him.

"Hello, son." Boss could smell his cologne and feel his presence drawing all the energy from the room and knew he wasn't hallucinating. His father was there in the flesh. Cadillac Bandz was alive!

Boss's guns felt too heavy to hold and fell to the floor. Cadillac, with his huge movie star like smile, opened his arms to embrace Boss. So many emotions flowed through Boss. He didn't know which to let take control of the situation. But the next thing he knew, his right fist was smashing into his father's jaw knocking him flat on his ass.

Rome chuckled and Tweety had a look of shock on her face.

Boss looked down at him with a scowling look. "You been alive this whole time?"

"Boss, I can explain," Cadillac said getting up off the floor, rubbing his jaw.

"Oh, you could explain why the man I've looked up to all my life faked his death to leave me to be raised by my mother? Or why you left the responsibility to me to take back the throne? Oh I gotta hear this!" Boss picked up his guns and pulled up a chair. He refilled his glass. Rome looked over at Cadillac and pointed to his watch. Cadillac nodded his head and wasted no time breaking everything done to Boss.

"Yo mama told me she already put you up on game about the fallout between me and Rome. But now dig these blues, Boss. The Phantom had been trying to move on me for a long time. Trying to get me to push his dope through the pimp game but anybody that know me knew I wasn't going to go for that shit. The dope game is poison to the pimp game and I respect this game way too much to fuck over it for a quick buck that I could get out of a hoe's butt.

The Phantom seen he couldn't get to me so he made plans to get rid of me. And the first person he came to to get the job done was Rome. Due to Rome's public display of a sucka attack and me banishing him from the game, everyone knew we were at odds. The Phantom came to Rome promising full reign of the pimp game if he pushed his dope for him. What the Phantom didn't know was despite our differences, Rome was loyal to me beyond measures. Rome told me everything. I contacted a friend of mines in the FBI and the three of us sat down and concocted a plan to get rid of the Phantom and keep you and your mother safe. Rome and I kept up the appearance of it being beef between us to keep everyone ignorant to what we were really on. Rome contacted Boom to plant a bomb on my boat and we faked my death.

I went into witness protection while Rome worked all these years to get all the evidence he could against the Phantom and everyone he's affiliated with."

Boss sat forward in his chair with a quizzical look on his face. "You saying you a snitch? You turned to the Feds to get rid of this nigga instead of taking him out yourself?"

"You don't know who the Phantom is, do you, Boss?" Rome interjected.

Boss shrugged his shoulders. "Does it matter who he is? He ain't a mythical creature. He a nigga that bleeds like I do."

"Yeah, but this nigga, son, has the full force of the police department and street thugs alike on his side. The Phantom is Aaron."

"The chief?"

Tweety nodded. "This just became news to me also."

"The only way to take down someone that powerful is with a force just is powerful. Which is why I called my friend in the FBI. Tonight was supposed to be the night everything came to an end. After this pick up, the Feds would have all the evidence they needed against The Phantom and his people. That's why it was important for you to return the money. That and I didn't want you to end up like Eric Wise."

"The dude those detectives killed? What did he have to do with this?"

"Eric, stole a bag of money out of the Chief's truck not knowing who it belonged to, just on some come up shit and gunned his ass down."

"Cadillac, it's time to roll, baby," Rome said pointing to his watch again. Cadillac nodded then turned his attention back to Boss. He put his hand on his shoulder.

"We got to go, but we going to do some catching up in a few hours when this is all over," Cadillac said as he checked the clips on his 9mm's.

"I'm coming with you."

"No, I need you here keeping your mama and your family safe until I get back."

"I'll have Uncle Fleetwood look after them."

"Fleetwood? Fleetwood works for the Phantom!"

"What! He's got Queenie and Lil Boss is with him right now!"

"You told him what you were doing here?"

"Yes." Just then they all knew Phantom was coming to them.

Boss called Fleetwood's phone and got no answer. A reminder on his phone showed he still had an unchecked email. Hoping it was something to do with Queenie and Lil Boss, he opened it up. The text read:

Boss, this is Princess. I know I'm the last person you want to hear from but this is a matter of life and death. I chose Polo at the challenge to protect you and the family. A few days before the picnic, Polo rolled down on me at the club showing me pics of you and Lil Boss out and about in different places. He was showing me he had eyes on us at all times. He's not working alone and Rome is not the force behind him. He's working a double-cross on Rome. Polo's working for the Phantom and the Phantom promised him the throne. They plan on getting rid of Rome at the time of the drop. They wanted to get rid of you unless I agreed to choose up to him when he challenged you. But Polo is now going against his word and plan on carrying out his hit on you. Please try understand that I only did this because I love you. Be careful Boss...

Boss got ready to tell all of them about the text message but was cut short by the door bursting open. It was too late, the drama had already arrived.

Chapter 23

Wayne listened in from the other side of the wall while the couple next in the bed next to him had sex.

SMACK!

Wayne smacked Helen on the ass real hard while Carl hit her shy and tenderly from the back. "Come on mane, smack her ass, pull her, fuck her like she's a whore and not your wife." Wayne coached the man.

"Oooooh Yessss!" Helen moaned loudly as she threw her ass back at Carl. "Hey, Mister Long John, won't you stop listening in on what's going on in the room next door and come show my husband how it's really done." Carl looked at her disappointingly, knowing he wasn't pleasing her.

"Maybe some other time, baby. Right now, I'm on business," Wayne said as he put his ear back to the wall to listen. What he was hearing had him even more on point. He phoned Sushi for her Lo and Vang to get to the hotel ASAP!

Sliding the phone back into his pocket, Wayne heard the door next door come crashing open. "What in the world was that!" Carl said from behind Helen's small flat bent over ass. Wayne pulled out his 44 magnum. "Jesus Christ! What's that for?" Carl yelled, while cowardly crawling on his ass away from Wayne to the wall on the other side of the room leaving Helen on the bed clutching the sheets in fear.

"Yo, be cool! This ain't for y'all." Wayne passed Carl on his way to the door, Carl curled up into a ball scared Wayne was going to hurt him. Wayne quietly opened the door and peered down the hallway both ways before heading next door. From what he was hearing, the shit was deeper than an ocean of mud. But it wasn't thicker than blood.

**

The door crashed opened followed by two cans of tear gas. The cans of tear gas went off with a loud bang before expelling fogs of tear gas. Boss covered his mouth and nose with his shirt and fired shots at the door. Choking off the gas, Hannah, tossed Rome the AK-47 from under the pillows before hitting the floor.

One of the police officers, Officer Jackson, on the Chief's payroll came in first wearing a gas mask over his face. Next, Detective Shaw, staying low came in firing shots in Rome's direction. Rome took aim at Shaw, letting loose a chain of bullets in his direction. Shaw took the little cover he could get behind a mini fridge. It was enough cover to give him temporary protection.

BOOM! CLICK! CLICK! BOOM!

Detective Perkins came in busting a twelve gauge shotgun, splintering a leg off one of the chairs in the room.

"Cadillac! We got to get out of here! I can't breathe!" Tweety yelled through a fit of coughs.

Cadillac was crouched on the floor next to Tweety. All five of them were taking cover by the bed. The room was filled with the fog of tear gas making visibility almost obsolete. But, Cadillac remembered the table was only a few feet away.

"Boss! Rome! Cover me!" He yelled to the other side of him. He crawled over to the table and put his hand up there to feel around. His hand hit something soft and slightly damp. He gripped it and snatched it down. It was what he was looking for. It was the towel Rome dried his hands off with earlier. He put his hand back on the table to feel around for the other thing he was looking for. His hand got close to

touching another item on the table. "Ahh shit!" A bullet flew pass scattering glass making him yank his hand back. Luckily it was the bottle of Louie 13 the bullet had tore through and not the item he was looking for.

He put his hand back on the table surfing the surface for the last item. His hand touched a plastic bottle. He quickly took hold of it. It was a bottle Fiji water Hannah was drinking on earlier.

He open the bottled water and poured it all over the towel. He covered Tweety's mouth and nose with the towel. "Rome, bust that damn window out and let's get some air in here!" Rome, not wanting to waste what little ammo he had, crawled over to the window with a splintered leg from the broken chair. One hard whack and the glass window shattered open. The fresh air coming in immediately began giving mercy to their lungs and eyes.

The foggy air was clearing out and the room was becoming visible again. Volleys of shots went back and forward. Boss caught Officer Jackson trying to advance on Cadillac and fired two shots at him one of them pierced his gas mask went into his left cheek and came out the right side of his head.

Rome checked the clip on his assault rifle. "Shit, I'm out!"

Cadillac fired four shots at Shaw. The slides of his guns slid back showing they were empty. "I'm out too! Boss, what got left?"

The slide was slid back on one of his guns. He checked the clip on the other. "Damn! It's only three left."

Sirens and the sound of tires screeching to a stop out front could be heard in the room. "You hear that Rome? That's the sound of your casket closing," Detective Perkins said as he loaded more shells into his twelve gauge. Part of the top of Boss's head was visible from his position behind the bed. It was a small part but it was all an excellent marksman like Shaw needed to hit his target. His finger wrapped around the trigger. He squinted his left eye then *BANG!*

From the top lip on up, Shaw's head was gone. Fragments of his face and head were all over the room. Wayne's 44 magnum still smoking, took aim at Perkins who was still loading the gauge. Perkins cocked the shotgun but had no time to take aim. Wayne sent five shots howling his way, laying Perkins flat out on the ground. " Come on! Let's go, let's go!" Wayne said waving everybody out the room. Boss picked up the money and dope and was the last out. He looked at Wayne.

"What took you so long?"

"My shoes was untied." They both chuckled.

Inside the hallway, they made their way to the elevators. Hannah frantically pressed the elevator button. The elevator could be heard approaching their floor. "One Adam twelve, we need all available officers at the Ambassador Hotel on Wisconsin." Chattered from an officer's walkie-talkie on the elevator that was approaching their floor.

"Shit! We got to take the stairs." Rome, with the whole party behind him, ran to the door that lead to the stairs. He swung open the door and was face to face with the barrel of a Mac 11.

"Whoaaa, easy baby, he with us," Wayne said pushing Sushi's gun away. "What it look like out there?"

"Police almost got the whole building surrounded."

"You say almost?"

"It's a back door in the kitchen that leads to out back. Follow me."

"Wait, where's Lo and Vang?" Sushi's stern face cracked a smile.

"Taking care of all unnecessary surprises with some surprises of their own." The elevator doors chimed.

"Go, go, go!" Boss ushered everyone down the stairs.

They get to the first floor. The lobby was swarming with the boys in blue. The kitchen was across the lobby from where they were.

Chief Aaron was on the other side of the wall where they were posted up at. He could be heard conversing with Detective Villa, another detective on his payroll. "Make sure you get the money and dope and they are not to get out of here alive. You understand?"

"Aye, papi, I got you." Detective Villa replied while slicking his salt and pepper hair back.

"Then go!" Villa went to the elevators and Chief Aaron went to the front desk.

Tweety peeped out the door of the stairwell. "How do we suppose to get out of here? They are everywhere."

Sushi pulled out her cellphone. "Yo, where y'all at?...alright, hurry up." She looked back at them. "Get ready to run out of here then through those kitchen doors" She pointed across the way from them. "Then straight out the back." They all braced themselves, ready to go when Sushi gave them the go head.

A large crowd of protesters came marching into the hotel. "NO JUSTICE, NO PEACE! NO RACIST ASS POLICE!" They chanted making their way into the small lobby.

Chief Aaron spent around. "Who let them past the yellow tape? Everyone out! He shouted at the crowd.

"Alright, run!" They jetted out the stairwell, ran through the kitchen doors and burst out the back door. They ran to the Taco Bell next door where Lo and Vang was waiting in the parking lot in a Blue's Clue daycare van. They all hopped inside. Lo smashed on the gas spinning the tires racing the van to the entrance of the alley. A fleet of squad cars came blocking off all traffic coming and going.

Sushi leaned towards the front seat. "Vang, do yo thang!" Vang got out and went to the back of the van. He opened the doors of the van and removed four drones with packages attached to the bottom of them. He sat the drones in front of the van then got back inside. Vang keyed some numbers into his phone and one of the drones came alive. They all huddled together and watched the video footage on Vang's phone of the drone flying to the right side of the hotel. It landed on the sidewalk next to the hotel. Vang pressed a button on the screen then an explosion went off and the footage went out. People screamed and scattered everywhere.

Vang started the next drone and flew it to the left side of the building setting off another explosion.

"Go!" Vang ordered Lo. Lo smashed out the parking lot. Vang flew the third drone, landing it on one of the squad cars that blocked off the intersection of 27th Street. The explosion of the third bomb caused the whole chain of squad cars to go up in flames. Lo busted a left on 27th Street.

Up ahead was another barricade of cars blocking the entrance to the highway. Vang dialed up the fourth drone sending it that way. The drone lost signal and crashed landed between two of the squad cars at the barricade. Boss seen the blank screen on Vang's phone.

"What you waiting on? Blow the mothafucka up!"

"I can't, I lost signal!" Vang told him slapping the phone with his hand.

"I guess yo smart phone on some stupid shit. That's gotdamn technology for yo' ass. Watch out, I'll take care of it the old fashion way." Cadillac climbed from the rear seat to the middle section. He opened the side sliding door. "Boss, toss me your gun."

Boss handed him his heat. Cadillac took aim at the package and fired. The shot missed by over two feet. The police officers got out their vehicles and returned fire. Lo swerved the van trying to dodge the parade of shots. Cadillac fired another shot missing this time by half a foot.

"Gotdamn Cadillac, you need glasses or something? What's wrong, you done got too old and lost yo' touch?" Cadillac gave Rome a stern look then fired another shot.

BOOM!

The shot nailed the small package of C4. The explosion made the two squad cars do wheelies and land upside down, taking out the police officers in the midst. Cadillac looked at Rome and smirked.

"Fuck what you talking 'bout, I still got it." Lo smashed right through the burnt wreckage and onto the highway.

Chapter 24

The crowd of choking, screaming protestors and guests came pouring out of the hotel doors. Smoke detectors, fire and car alarms all throughout the area were going haywire. The explosions left holes on in the sidewalk, the side of the hotel and in the city street. Ashes, smoke and debris filled the air. Police didn't know what to do. The whole scene was chaos.

Chief Aaron, with a handkerchief folded across his mouth, pushed his way through the crowd in the lobby to where one of his officers stood directing the crowd of people to the exits.

"Jefferson! You want to tell me what the hell is going on!" Jefferson was a world class dumb ass, good for nothing more than directing traffic. The Chief still ed him anyway in hopes that maybe this time he would have a valuable answer for him.

"I believe it was an explosion sir." The minute Jefferson opened his mouth, he regretted even talking to him. If it wasn't for him being a good send off, the chief would've been got rid of him.

"I know it was an explosion you idiot, who set it?"

Jefferson shrugged. The chief wanted to put his foot up Jefferson's dumb ass but he didn't have the time to waste. "Do you have your radio?"

"Yes sir."

"Give it to me!" Jefferson hands his radio to him. The chief lost his walkie-talkie somewhere in the crowd of people when the explosion went off, knocking him to the floor. "Villa, come in."

"Go head, Chief."

"Did you catch the suspects? Over."

"No, they got away chief. Over."

"Gotdamit, what room are you in? Over."

"303, but if I were you I would take the stairs. That explosion did a number on the elevator. Over." The chief put the walkie-talkie in the radio holster on his waist.

"Um, chief."

"What!"

Jefferson cleared his throat nervously. "My radio?"

The chief noticed he was cuffing Jefferson's radio by mistake. He took it back out of his holster and tossed back to him. Then, he pushed his way through the crowd once more making his way to the stairwell.

Out of breath from running up just three flights of stairs, the chief's age was catching up to him. Though he still had the appearance of an athletic physique, the chief wasn't as fast and agile as he was ten years ago when he was in his thirties.

He wiped the sweat from his brow with his handkerchief and eased his breathing before walking into room 303. He never displayed such weakness in front of anyone, afraid they might try him. In his book, respect is first giving to that that is feared before giving to that that is loved.

The walls inside the room was dotted with bullet holes. Chairs were scattered around the room in sticks and splinters. A lite breeze came through the busted out window. The chief looked to his left and seen what was left of Detective Shaw. His torso and what was left of his head laid sprawled across the mini fridge while the rest of his head decorated the room. Flies gathered around a puddle of Shaw's blood and brain matter. Glass under the chief's shoe made a crunching sound when he treaded towards the area the table sat.

Villa strolled into the room. "They made quite the mess in here, chief. I just came from the couple's room next door. They say another man was posted up in their room listening in on what was going on in here before running out of there with a gun in his hand."

"What about my money?"

"Gone, sir," Villa said walking over to where Perkin's body laid. Villa nudged the body over onto it's back with his foot. Perkins grumbled making Villa jump back in surprise that he was still alive.

The chief heard it too. He rushed over to Perkin's side. The chief ripped opened Perkin's shirt. There were five large, mangled, caliber slugs lodged into his bulletproof vest.

"Sit him up!" The chief grabbed one arm and Villa, with a cigarette dangling from between his lips, took ahold of the other arm and they set Perkins upwards. "Perkins, what went down in here?"

Perkins was sore and in pain from the bullets of Wayne's 44 hitting his vest so hard they fractured three of his ribs and bruised majority of his torso. The impact of the shots had knocked him unconscious.

"Six."

"Six? Six what?" Perkins faded out again from the pain of the broken ribs. The chief slaps him a couple times on the face. "Perkins, focus! Six what?" The whole room spinning but he was forcing himself to regain his focus.

"There were six of them."

Two other officers approached the room with cops of coffee in their hands laughing at a joke one told the other.

"GET THE HELL OUT OF HERE! Man the fucking hallway and let no one through that door!" The chief ordered the two officers. The malice in his voice wiped the smiles off their faces.

"Yes, sir." The officers closed the door behind them. The chief returned to questioning Villa.

"Six of them?" Villa asked. Perkins, now gaining back his composure, reached across his body unclamping the clips on each side releasing the tight grasp of his vest against his torso. He pulled the vest off over his head then threw it across the room. He snatched the cigarette out of Villa's mouth taking a hard pull of it before continuing.

"There were six of them. Rome, his bitch Hannah, that punk bitch Tweety, Boss and two other dudes I don't know." He took another hit of the cigarette and expelled a train of smoke from his nostrils. "One of the dudes was an older man. He kept Tweety shielded while we exchanged gunfire. The other guy came out of nowhere. He caught Shaw from behind while I was loading my shotgun. I didn't have time to get a shot off before he squeezed off five rounds into my vest. I don't know what happened after that, I was out cold. Believe me Phantom, I tried my best to get them. They had us outnumbered."

The chief stood up and scrolled over to the busted out window. With his back to them he screwed a silencer onto his PP7 pistol. "You did what you could, right?"

"I did."

"Too bad it wasn't good enough."

PEWWW! PEWWW! Two bullets swiftly whispered out of the barrel of the PP7 and into Perkins skull.

"JESUS!" Villa, caught by surprise that the chief shot Perkins, jumped back from Perkins' lifeless body. "Holy shit! You almost shot me."

The chief tucked his gun away. "You disappoint me too and it won't be no almost. Yo ass will be funking up the morgue next to their ass. Comprende?" Villa swallowed hard and nodded. "Now, put a BOLO out on both Rome and Boss.

The chief's phone rang. It was Boss's number that appeared on the screen.

"Boss, what can I do for you?"

"You can give me back my wife and kid."

"Your wife and kid is missing?" The chief wasn't sure if Boss found out or not that he was the Phantom so he decided to play it by ear.

"You can cut the shit, Phantom! My uncle Big Hunnid is one of your flunkies. He's holding my family hostage for you and I want them back!" A sly smile styled the chief's face. Being confronted by Boss made him feel like a wolf coming out of sheep clothing.

"Rome and his biggg mouth. Well, if you know that then you must have what I'm looking for. Fair exchange wouldn't be robbery. Meet me at—"

"No, I'll name the place and time. I don't trust you not to have some sort of surprise awaiting me."

"I see. Then, where and when?"

"Meet me at Churchill Apartments on 29th and Wisconsin Avenue at one in the morning. Oh, and make sure Big Hunnid is present."

"Will do." The chief ended the call. "Villa, cancel that BOLO. We already know where they're going to be. It's four of them—"

"No, Perkins said it was six of them."

"I'm not worried about the two bitches. Get some of our men together. Sneak out some of those heavy weapons from the evidence room we confiscated in last week's raid on the Meadows. Then, meet up with me at the McDonald's on 25th and Wisconsin Avenue."

"You got it, chief."

The chief opened the door. "Keep the media away from here and get forensics in here ASAP!" The chief told the two officers standing outside.

"Right away, sir," One of the officers said scrambling away to go find the forensic team while the other officer went in the other direction to keep the media from getting past the yellow tape outside.

If Boss thought this was gonna be a smooth transaction then he had another thing coming. They knew who the Phantom was the chief and he had no plans on letting any of them walk out of there alive. But little did the chief know, Boss had a plan of his own.

***

Isis was instructing Macita, Sapphire and Gemini on what to do when they get to Miami when the front door opened. Boss walked in followed by Tweety, Cadillac then Rome and Hannah. When Isis seen Rome, she went for her purse removing F&N pistol from it. The beam from the pistol glowed a bright red dot on his forehead.

"Bitch, you dare point a gun at me." Boss stepped into the line of fire.

"It's good baby, put it away."

"What is he doing here, Boss?"

"Big Hunnid's got Lil Boss and Queenie. Rome's going to help us get them back."

"Your uncle kidnapped them?"

"Yeah. He's working for the Phantom." Boss explained the whole story to them and letting them know who the Phantom was so they'd know exactly what they were up against. Then, he put them onto the plan he had in mind. All that was left to do was to execute it.

Chapter 25

Boss looked out the window of the fifth floor then radioed the car that just arrived. It was Vang and Lo. After ditching the daycare van, they parked two stolen Hayabusa motorcycles on the side of an apartment building directly across the street from Churchill Apartments. "I see y'all. Keep the car running and wait for my signal."

"Got you," Lo, radioed back.

Boss chirped Wayne. "Wayne, where you at?"

"Me and Sushi getting into position now," Wayne chirped back. Sushi pulled up in the Audi R8 and parked on the side of Churchill Apartments. Wayne, sat on the passenger side loading a 32 round clip into a SKS. Sushi stopped him.

"No, bae. Load the Mickey Mouse ears on to it. You know how I love to sweep shit," she said while holding the weed smoke in her lungs. Wayne shook his head and smiled. He loved how gangsta his girl was. It wasn't no one he trusted more to fight by his side than her.

He put the 32 round clip to the side and stuck in a 200 round double drum clip into it. He passed it to her then grabbed a M-16 from the backseat. He loaded a guerrilla's nuts clip into it. It was 200 round double drum clip the same as the Mickey Mouse ears but he liked the name guerilla nuts better. Mickey Mouse ears sounded too cute for gangsta like him.

Boss, radioed Isis. "Isis, everythang's everythang?"

She chirped back instantly. "We're all set, daddy."

The chief's Ford F150 pickup truck pulled up in front of the apartment building blocking the bus stop. A blacked out Durango pulled up behind him. Out came Detective Villa slicking back his hair with a small black comb. The back door of the Durango opened and Big Hunnid stepped out with Lil Boss in one hand and yanking Queenie out the car with his other.

Boss sat the radio down on the window sill then turned to face Rome and Cadillac. "They're here. Y'all ready for this?"

"I don't believe we have a choice but to be," Rome said.

"Pops, what are you doing?" "I'll explain…it to you in one…second." Cadillac was heating up a pocket knife with a Zippo lighter. Then, he used it to take a part his iPhone. The heated knife melted through the adhesive, used to seal the phone and it's back covering together, like butter. Once the back was off, he removed the battery and took a small chip out the handkerchief in suit jacket and held it up for them to see.

"When I went into the witness protection, the Feds relocated me to Wilsonville, Oregon. They set me up in a modest condominium and gave me this phone to keep track of me. I took this tracking device out the phone and powered it off. They haven't heard from me in two days now, I know they looking. I'm putting it back in so they'll know…exactly…where…to find me," He said as he finished placing the chip back into the phone. Cadillac reattached the back of the phone then powered it on. The screen went red filling up with a bunch of scrambled numbers and letters then rebooting itself to a normal screensaver. "Alright, let's get this show on the road."

The chief was the first to reach the door that lead to the lobby of the apartments. The lobby doors were locked. Isis came to the door with Gemini and Sapphire behind her with Dracos trained on the chief and Big Hunnid. She opened the door to let them in. The chief came in looking at the scowling face women with a sly smile. "Is all the weapons necessary?"

"You can stop right there," Isis ordered them. "I'll take your weapons gentlemen."

"What if we refuse?" Big Hunnid asked walking up on her but stopped dead in his tracks as all the girls pointed their guns at his head.

"Then, you better pray there's a heaven for a washed up P."

"It's alright, Big Hunnid. Give them your piece."

Reluctantly, Big Hunnid handed over his Berretta.

"Now your turn."

The chief reached inside his jacket for his two service Glocks inside his holsters.

"Slowly! Or I'll blow your head off!"

"Easy there, sweetheart." The chief slowly took off his jacket then holsters and handed them to Isis. "There, now can we go take care of business?"

"Macita, check them."

"Is that really necessary?"

Thoroughly!" She commanded her while staring at the chief. Assuming the position, the chief had spread his legs apart and held his arms out. A position he was used to putting others in. Macita's hands scrolled roughly over his torso to his waist then down his legs where she found a snub nose 38 in his ankle holster. "Let me guess, you forgot you had that on you?" The chief gave her the same sly grin he gave her when he first walked in.

"Take the elevator to the fifth floor. When you get off, go to room 502. And if you think about pulling any kind of stunts up there, you might as well tell me what funeral home to ship your bodies too. Because neither of you will make it out of here alive."

The elevator dinged and doors opened up. Big Hunnid, still holding Lil Boss, pushed Queenie inside the elevator and then the chief got inside. The chief pressed the button for the fifth floor.

"You call Serenity Funeral home for me. That Randy Guy does great work there," the chief said and laughed as the elevator doors closed.

Inside the elevator, the chief sent a text to his crew informing them which apartment the exchange would be taking place in. Villa texted back immediately telling him they were less than a minute away from getting into position. He put his phone away and caught a side glance at Queenie staring at him blankly. He rubbed the knuckle of his pointer finger down the side of her face. His eyes fell on her round bubble butt.

"What a shame. All that going on in the basement and yet the attic is empty as hell. So much woman and not a lick of brains left in her."

Her eyes watered as his hand traced down her back. Lil Boss woke up whining before his hand made it to her butt.

"Aww, come here lil man." The chief took him from Big Hunnid. The elevators binged. The doors slid open and they walked out of the elevators turning right then made an immediate left turn that lead them to apartment 502.

Big Hunnid tapped a few times at the door and it came open. Boss answered. When he saw Queenie, he took her in his arms and squeezed her tight. "Baby, you okay?" He asked her while his examined her body for any bruises or harm. Then, he reached for Lil Boss. The chief snatched Lil Boss away from his reach. Boss, Cadillac and Rome pointed their guns at the chief and Big Hunnid. The chief waved his finger at Boss.

"No, no, no. Business first. Where's my money?"

The apartment was small. The tiny kitchen was connected to the living room. Around the corner from the living room was a small bathroom and next to that was the apartment's only bedroom. The apartment was empty except for a wobbly wood table that sat in the living room, a dusty old refrigerator that smelled like mold and the cheap office chair Cadillac was sitting in. The kitchen faucet spoked in slow drips. No electricity inside the apartment, the whole thing was lit up by moonlight that poured in from the big picture window in the front room.

Cadillac's chair was facing the window putting his back towards them. To them, it looked as if he was texting on his phone. Little do they know he was watching their every move. Their reflection appeared to him on the dark screen of his phone. Rome stood in front of Cadillac's chair concealing his identity that much more.

"I got your money close by."

"It's not in my hands so it ain't close enough."

"You going to get your money soon enough."

"What's the hold up?"

"Somebody wants to talk to you first." Rome stepped out of the way and Cadillac spent around in his chair.

"Chief Aaron. Or should I call you Phantom. Remember me?" Big Hunnid raced laps in his chest he saw Cadillac alive after all those years. The chief's eyes nearly bulged from his head in shock.

"You supposed to be dead." His attention then fell upon Rome. "Why isn't this man dead?" The chief's brief moment of shock washed over as fast as it came after quickly putting things together. "You been playing me, Rome?"

"Look here Phantom, I would tell you it's just business, but nah." Rome's face balled into a mean mug. "This shit here is personal."

The chief was a power hungry bastard that enjoyed the art of controlling other people. Seeing Rome wasn't in his control made his blood boil.

"Rome and I been like brothers since we were knee high to grasshoppers. The love for your bro outweighs the love of a hoe. You couldn't really expect him to do me in, did you?"

"Why not? Tell me what man wouldn't kill anyone they had to for money and power? I offered yo' bitch ass an opportunity of a lifetime. All you had to do is kill Cadillac and have those dumb whores push my dope and the pimp game was yours. I held up my end of the bargain. I even used both my police and street resources to get rid of anyone who ever tried to come for your position. I would've took out Boss if it wasn't for you telling me you had him. Did all that for yo po pimping ass and you play me? You a dead man. Every breath you breathe from this moment on is borrowed time!" The chief cut his eyes to Boss. "Bring me my money before I lose my temper and things get real ugly in here."

"I don't believe you are in any predicament to be giving demands. We got the guns and there is more of us than there is of you. What's keeping me from putting a bullet in y'all heads and taking my wife and kid back?"

"Your father. Cadillac and Rome both know I'm not stupid enough to come here alone." The chief held Lil Boss up. On the rooftop of an apartment building cross the street, Villa watched with night vision goggles what was going on inside the apartment. He spoke to the sniper lying on the rooftop peering through the scope of a rifle.

"The chief gave the signal." The sniper squeezed the trigger. A silencer mounted on the barrel freed the bullet without a bang. The bullet flew inches above Lil Boss's head and embedded into the wall near the front door. Everyone ducked.

"Whoaaa! Wait a minute! You want yo' money, I got you. But you got to let my wife and kid go first."

"Where's my money?"

Boss held up a finger telling him to wait a minute. He called Lo and told him to hold up the cash. He called the chief over to the window. Cautiously, he went to the window and peered out. Lo and Vang had the bags of money lying on the gas tanks of their motorcycles and held up bundles of cash in their hands.

"Let them go and my boys will leave the money in the bed of your truck."

The chief shook his head. "Nah, let's readvise your plan a little. You have your boys drop off the bags in my truck bed.

My boys come pick it up and if everything's all there then I'll let your bitch and brat go."

Still standing in the window, Boss looked down at Vang and Lo and rubbed his nose. They pulled off.

"Why would we do that? We both know you have no reason to keep us alive after you get your money," Rome told him.

"True, I have every reason to kill all of you. You know who I am, you played with my money and caused me a whole lot of trouble. Though you have my word, that everyone will walk out of here alive."

"Fine, we'll do things your way." Boss called Lo and Vang back and told them to make the drop off.

"I hope you know what you're doing, or we all dead." Cadillac whispered to Boss. Big Hunnid lit up a cigarette which drew Cadillac's attention his way. "Still smoking those little white dicks I see."

"Old habits are hard to quit." Big Hunnid shook a match extinguishing the flame.

"Indeed, they are. For the weak at least. It's funny how the weak always want to control everything but can't control their own self. Answer me the obvious question. Why would you betray your own family?"

"Why else? I needed the money, Cadillac. Dope game was washing my pimping out. Most of the whores were strung out. It was mo' money for me in selling dope than a bitch. Add in the fact I owed a huge gambling debt. I had to do what was necessary to survive and you just happened to be in the way of my survival."

"You a real piece of shit, Big Hunnid. It's going to be a pleasure to take a piss on yo grave."

Big Hunnid's response was interrupted by the hum of Vang and Lo's motorcycles pulling up to the chief's pickup. The chief stood next to Boss in the window. Vang and Lo tossed their bag in the bed of the truck and took off.

The chief made a call to his men to come pick it up. It didn't take long for one of his men to come out of the apartment building next door to his truck. When Boss seen the man come out of the apartment building next door, he figured with the chief having men across the street and next door he must have them surrounding the whole area. That meant Boss and his people would have to stay alert if they were going to make it out of there alive.

The man opened the bags looked up at the window and nodded his head to the chief.

Okay, you got your money now let us go."

"A deal is a deal. Y'all free to go. But to ensure I make out of here without a bullet in the back of my head, I'm not giving you yo' kid until I'm out of this building."

Holding no objections to the chief's wish, they all filed out of the apartment behind the chief. They stopped at the elevator waiting for it to reach their floor. Lil Boss began to fuss.

"Shh, shh, shhh," The chief sang to him as he patted him and bounced him in his arms. Boss kept a close eye on the chief but not close enough to see him slip his hand up the back of Lil Boss's shirt. The elevator dinged. Faster than the blink of an eye, the chief had pulled out a .380 and fired a shot that struck Cadillac in the shoulder. Boss helped Queenie to cover around the corner from the elevator while Rome helped Cadillac. Big Hunnid and the chief, still holding Lil Boss, got into the elevator. Rome got a couple of shots before Boss stopped him.

"Rome stop shooting, my son's in there!"

"Shit!" Rome wanted to knock the Phantom's head off his shoulders. He'd been waiting for the moment to do so since he'd first started working for the Phantom.

"Big Hunnid! Get this elevator to the rooftop!" Big Hunnid pressed the button furiously.

"I'm trying! This raggedy mothafucking button stuck!" The chief let off two more shots in Boss's direction.

"I knew your bitch ass wasn't going to keep your word, Phantom!" Rome yelled.

"How come I didn't? I said y'all would make it out of the apartment alive and y'all did. I didn't say nothing about what would happen afterwards." He laughed then pushed Big Hunnid out the way. After few pounds on the button with his fist, the doors started to close.

Cadillac held his shoulders peeping around the corner at the closing elevator doors. "We can't let them make it to the rooftop. He'll have that sniper covering him until his boys swarm this building, taking us all out." Queenie let out a loud scream that made them all turn their heads in her direction. She laid squirming on the floor. Her pants were soak and wet. Her water had broke.

"She's going into labor!" Boss rushed towards her. Cadillac stopped him.

"Boss, go stop that elevator."

"I got to help my wife!" He tried to push pass but Cadillac's grip was too strong.

"No, focus! You got to stop that elevator. If not none of us, not your wife or that child she's having is going to make it out of here alive. Neither me nor Rome are fast enough to run up them steps to stop that elevator. We'll get her to the lobby so the girls can get her to the hospital. Now GO!"

Boss bit his bottom lip hard as if biting back his own stubbornness to do what was more practical. Then, he took off up the four flights of stairs. He seized a fire extinguisher from the stairwell. When he made it to the elevator, it was already two floors away from arriving. Boss repeatedly slammed the butt of the fire extinguisher into the bottom and top of the elevator doors. Dents formed into the doors. The elevator was almost there. Boss pounded harder and faster and after three more hits, the elevator doors became bent inwards and off the track. Just in time as the elevator was leaving the eighth floor the floor before the rooftop. Though the bent in doors kept it from going up any further, Boss could hear the chief and Big Hunnid inside pressing the button. The chief was becoming agitated. Boss heard him call up one of his men telling them it was a change in plans and that they were going to leave out through the garage. Boss rushed back downstairs to Queenie.

Queenie was balled up on the floors screaming through her contraction pain. The girls tried to calm her down. "Why haven't y'all got her to the car?"

"We're waiting on Hannah to bend the corner." The tires of Hannah's BMW screeched to a stop out front.

"There she go now," Rome said opening the lobby door. Boss scooped Queenie up off the floor.

Hannah got out the truck to open her back door for them. "Hurry!" Hannah waved them over. Boss ran towards the car with Queenie crying in his arms holding her stomach. The rest of the crew followed behind him watching his six. "Hurry! Hur-"

PEWWW!

A 50 caliber bullet from the sniper's rifle whistled through the air, scattering confetti size pieces of Hannah's head everywhere. Though Boss was fifteen feet away, the explosion of Hannah's skull still managed to splatter blood and brain matter onto him and Queenie. None of them had a chance to give a reaction to what had just happened before a squad of nine of Phantom's men popped out from some of everywhere blasting at them. Not able to reach Hannah's truck, they fled back into the building. The closer the shooters got to the building, they formed a triangular formation, rotating shooters to keep a constant shower of bullets raining into the building and keeping the people inside from being able to bust back.

Boss ducked low next to a wall in the lobby. He shielded Queenie as bullets flew passed and glass rained on them. He was mad at his self for forgetting the radio on the windowsill.

"Where the hell is Wayne! I know he hear these bastards shooting at us!"

***

"You got it baby?" Wayne asked, handing Sushi her riffle.

"Yup." She strapped the riffle around her shoulder, gave Wayne a peck on the lips and put a blueberry Blow Pop in her mouth. Sushi scaled the ladder behind the apartment building across the street from Churchill Apartments. She caught sight of the sniper on the roof. He was in position peering through the scope of his rifle while talking into an earpiece attached to his left ear. She stalked closer to him. Her hands slipped into her hair and slipped back out with two, long, sharp, knitting needles.

The sniper didn't see it coming. Sushi jumped on his back sticking the first needle below his neck into his spinal cord, paralyzing him on impact. She moved with lighting speed wasting no time lodging the other one in his right ear, killing him. Sushi tossed her Blow Pop off the side of the building then picked up the sniper riffle and took aim at Phantom's men.

Wayne received Sushi's signal when the sucker hit the ground in front of him. Without a moment to spare, he ran blasting his way towards Churchill Apartments. One squeeze of the trigger on Wayne's M-16 and bullets were spiting up like a bulimic with a finger in her throat. The surprise attack caused Phantom's men to break formation. Taking their concentration, for brief moment, off the targets inside the apartment lobby gave Boss people a chance to bust back at them.

Wayne crouched down behind an abandoned black Acura. Four of the nine men concentrated their fire on Wayne while the remaining five took cover against the building exchanging shots with the people inside. When the shooting paused inside the building, one of the men attempted to advance inside. His foot didn't make it past the threshold. Sushi put a bullet through his collarbone that traveled down to his heart and exited out, lodging into one of the mailboxes in the lobby. Seeing their sniper had been compromised, the rest of the men scattered for cover.

"Yeah, run like lil bitches," Sushi said to herself with a grin.

Most women would've been terrified being in the middle of a shootout but not Sushi, she was having the time of her life.

***

Gemini and Sapphire were changing out their empty magazine clips when Sushi took out the man that was attempting to enter the building. Boss was doing his best to hold onto Queenie who was screaming and squirming in his arms. "We got to get to Hannah's truck, now."

"What about Phantom? He's gonna get away. Did you forget he still has your son?" Rome questioned Boss.

"He won't go too far when he finds out I still got something he wants." Cadillac interjected.

"And what's that?"

Cadillac held up his iPhone. "After I turned my phone on upstairs, I hit record on it. Everything, and I mean everything I do with this phone they know about. Not only have the Feds been tracking us since I put that chip in, but they been also listening and recording everything that sucka ass nigga was admitting to upstairs. Get Queenie to the hospital then we'll take care of him."

"Isis, you drive. The rest of y'all cover us and get to the car as fast as you can."

Queenie let out a shrill scream causing all eyes to fall on her. A stream of blood ran down her legs. "Move out!" Boss ordered everyone.

The bullet riddled glass doors to the lobby shattered when Gemini pushed them open. She flipped a latch at the top of the door that held it open. Even more of Phantom's men showed up, greeting them with gunfire. Wayne and Sushi distracted as many as they could. Gemini and Sapphire shielded the front of Boss, Rome, Cadillac and Macita took up the rear.

They shot their way to the truck. The girls continued providing Boss and Queenie with cover while he got in the backseat with her. Isis jumped in the driver's seat, Gemini got in the backseat with Boss and Sapphire hopping in front. They heard the sirens and seen the flashing lights on the several blacked out Chevy Tahoes turning off 35th Street and coming down Wisconsin towards them.

"Boss, take this." Cadillac gave him the Fed phone with the recording. "Go get my grandson back. Rome and I will handle the Feds."

"Macita, get in. Let's go!" Isis yelled at Macita who was still popping shots off. Macita laid down one more then turned to squeeze into the backseat. Five shots struck her in the back.

"MACITA! NOOO!" Isis screamed. Cadillac caught the man with three shots to the torso that laid him out. Macita fell to her knees with blood pouring out her mouth. With her eyes on locked onto Boss's, she coughed out, "I'm sorry daddy. I love you." Macita's eyes rolled into the back of her head and she fell over dead. Boss closed his eyes for a brief moment. Queenie's scream brought him back to the moment's urgency.

"Isis! Bitch drive!"

Isis foot stomped on the gas pedal and off the block before the Feds made it to 29th Street.

Chapter 26

Tweety hung up her phone and waited patiently in her car up the street from Polo's crib. Her mind was filled with worry. She had yet to hear back from Boss and them since they left to do the exchange with the chief. All she could do at that point was pray that everything went as planned. She wanted to go with them but both Cadillac and Boss insisted that she go do what she had to do to get Princess. It wasn't going to be easy, this she knew. But she wasn't going to leave without her.

Tweety knocked on Polo's door. Kiwi opened the door, patting her weave, looking Tweety up and down. "Can I help you?" The tone of her voice was filled with sarcasm. Tweety wanted to check her. As a formal bottom bitch, she was used to dealing with smart mouth whores and she enjoyed putting them in their place. She didn't have the time for it at that moment. At that moment, it was more important matters at hand.

"Where's Polo?"

"He ain't here. He made a run with that girl Peaches. Why? What you want with Polo? You a little too old for his stable, ain't you?" Kiwi was still patting her weave. It was itching something terrible. Tweety was itching to make Kiwi swallow her teeth. Again though, she was stronger than her emotions and kept her focus on the bigger picture.

"Never mind that. Where's Princess?" Kiwi's natural reaction almost made her look behind her. Tweety caught her hesitation.

"I don't know who you talking about. Besides, I'm busy right now. Bye."

Tweety adjusted her purse strap on her shoulder then WHAM! She threw her shoulder into the door just as Kiwi was closing it, making it crash right into Kiwi's nose. Kiwi fell to the ground cursing holding her bloody nose.

Tweety went through the house room to room opening doors and yelling Princess's name. She came upon one bedroom door that was locked. It's door handle was replaced with a deadbolt lock. She was running her shoulder into the door when Kiwi came running up behind her with a rolling pin in hand. "Bitchhhh!"

Tweety withdrew her baby Desert Eagle from her purse and had it pointed at Kiwi's dome before she could get close enough to take a swing at her.

"Let me give yo young dumb ass some advice. The key to sneaking up on somebody is remaining silent."

Kiwi felt embarrassed for yelling bitch and messing up her sneak attack on Tweety. "Get yo stupid ass over here and open this door!"

Kiwi pulled the key out her pocket. With Tweety's gun to the back of her head, she unlocked the door. Inside, Princess was tied to a chair with a hair scarf tied around her mouth as a mouth gag. "Untie her!"

Squeezing her bloody nose, with the bottom of her shirt, she did what she was told. While Kiwi was untying Princess, Tweety removed her gag.

"Mama Bandz!" Princess face lit up at the site of Tweety.

"Boss got your message and sent me to come get you out of here."

Kiwi undid the last of Princess's restraints. Princess sprang to her feet rubbing her wrist, glad to be freed of her restraints.

Tweety pressed the gun against Kiwi's chest. "Sit yo ass in that chair. Princess, tie this skank up."

"With pleasure."

"Polo's going to kill y'all stupid bitches and that nigga Boss."

"Yeah but who you think he's gonna kill first for letting Princess get away?"

Kiwi eyes grew big when she realized Tweety was right. Polo wasn't going to be pleased with Princess getting away under her watch. Tweety gaged her mouth with the same scarf that was used to gag Princess.

Princess got up from tying her legs down. She looked down at Kiwi's head. "Ooh, you need to do something about that dry, irritated scalp. That come from putting cheap weave in your head. It looks like it itches something terrible."

Kiwi mumbled something through her gag while franticly trying to lean her head into her shoulder to scratch it.

Tweety and Princess left Kiwi crying to scratch her scalp and hit it to the crib to wait for further instructions.

Chapter 27

Queenie tossed and turned trying to wiggle her way free from the restraints the hospital staff put on her. The doctors and nurses were forced to restrain her to limit her movement for they could help deliver the baby. Boss held her hand and rubbed her head to calm her down but it wasn't working. Her pain was unbearable.

"Hurts, I hurts!" Was all she kept repeating.

The doctor came up from between her legs. The look on his face spoke volumes. The urgent manner in which he ordered the nurses around, heightened Boss's sense of worry. "Something wrong, doc?"

"Mr. Bandz, there's a problem with the delivery."

"What kind of problem?"

"The baby is breached. Your wife has lost a lot of blood and with her...mental disability, we can't make her understand that we need her to push to help get the baby out. If she don't push, we will have to do an emergency C-section."

"Okay, well do it"

"It's not that simple Mr. Bandz. It's a high probability that your wife might not make it if we do the C-section. With the amount of blood lost she's had, I'm afraid she's not going to survive us going in taking the baby out. The baby isn't far enough out the birth canal for us to get the clamps around its head to pull him out. Plus, she's too far along for us to give her an Epidural or anything else for the pain."

"What if she pushes the baby out far enough for you to get your clamps around its head. Then they'll both survive, right?"

"I suppose. But she isn't strong enough to do so and doesn't comprehend what we are telling her to do."

"Let me worry about that. You just get down there and get your tools ready."

The doctor shook his head then got to work ordering the nurses to get ready for a natural birth and to be on standby for a C-section.

"Queenie, baby, you got push this baby out. I know you can do it." His babying her wasn't working. Queenie wasn't listening to nothing he was saying. She was still squirming around crying out, getting weaker and weaker each time.

Boss grabbed her by the jawline with one hand. With a treacherous mug on his face and venom in his every word he said, "Look here Bitch!" The doctor and nurses looked at him in disgust for the way he was talking to his mentally challenged wife.

"Mr. Bandz! That is not necessary." Boss flashed his mug at them and they quickly backed off. His attention returned back to Queenie. "Now when you signed up to be my bitch, you promised to give me yo' all. When I married you, you vowed to give me even more than that. Don't you start cheating me out of our deal now. Hoe, you better push this baby out!" She stared at him a moment with tears in her eyes. Then, she shut her eyes tight and to the doctors and nurses amazement, Queenie was pushing. She was pushing so hard she was turning red and the veins in her forehead were showing.

"Good, good. You're doing great, Mrs. Bandz. Give us one more good push and I can get in there and maneuver the baby around and pull him out." Queenie pushed again but it was too feeble of a push to count. She was too weak to push any more. Boss unstrapped her restraints. Then, he wiped the sweat from her brow and pressed her harder.

"Don't you quit on me, Queenie. Push Gotdamit!" Her right hand gripped the railing, her left hand squeezed Boss's. Her teeth were clenched and her eyes tightly she shut.

"ARRRR! Ahhh!" She growled then screamed as she gave the biggest push she could give.

"That's good, that's good!" The doctor yelled. "I got her!" The next thing heard was the cries of the baby. "It's a girl!"

Boss leaned down and kissed Queenie's forehead. The doctors gave him the scissors to cut the umbilical cord.

The nurses cleaned the baby off and presented her to Queenie. Boss helped her hold her.

Queenie looked at the small bundle of joy in her arms. "Boo, baby." Boss couldn't refuse a smile from taking over his face. For a moment, starring down at his new baby girl he forgot all about the drama he was caught up in.

"You did it, baby," Boss said to Queenie. A smile was raising on her face but faded fast. Her eyes rolled into the back of her head. Her head fell back onto the mattress. Boss moved the baby away. The monitors in the room beeped loudly as Queenie flatlined. "Queenie?"

The doctor and nurses rushed over to her side. "What's wrong with my wife?"

"Sir, please wait outside," the head nurse told him while herding him out the door and taking the baby. Finding himself pacing the floor again while Queenie fights for her life was déjà vu all over again for Boss.

A half hour later, Tweety and Princess showed up at the hospital. They ran over to hug him. "Oh thank God you're alright. Did Queenie have baby?"

"Yeah, ma, she had her. She's down the hall in the nursery."

"It's a girl?"

Tweety was excited to hear she had a granddaughter. She darted off to the nursery with Boss and Princess trailing behind her.

"I'm so glad you got my message. Daddy, I don't know what I would've done if something happened to you. Was I wrong for choosing Polo to protect you and the family? I just can't help but feel like I disappointed you by doing so," Princess admitted on the walk to the nursery.

"You did what you had to do to look after the family. Because of that, most of us are still alive."

"Most?"

"Macita got killed during a shootout with the Phantom's people."

Princess gasped and put her hands over her mouth.

"Oh, no." Her mind wandered to the most important person in her life. "Where's Lil Boss?" They stopped in front of the glass windows of the nursery.

"Which one is my grandbaby?"

Boss was grateful for the moment of interruption. It was going to be hard for him to tell Princess about Lil Boss.

"The fifth one in the fourth row." Tweety caught sight of the new addition to the Bandz family. He hated to tell Princess but he had to.

Tweety turned around in horror of what she just heard. "Aaron's got Lil Boss?" Boss nodded his head.

"He's got my son and you're standing around the hospital enjoying being a proud father to your new baby girl?" Boss was so angered by her comment he could've bit her head off. But he understood her frustration and what it may have looked like to her, which is why he thought it would make best of the situation if he explained what was going on.

"You think I'm happy right now? Yeah, my baby girl was born and this should be one of the proudest moments in my life. But I can't enjoy it. Not while that maniac has my son and Queenie might be in there dead." He pointed down the hall. "I already set up the meet with him to get Lil Boss back. He wants me to meet him at 1:00 PM at the 7 Mile Fair swap meet."

"Wait a minute, back up. What you mean Queenie might be dead?" Boss explained to his mama and Princess everything that happened at Churchill Apartments and what happened to Queenie after she gave birth.

Tweety's phone rang just as the doctor walked in. "Mr. Bandz, I have good news. Your wife is stable and doing fine."

"What happened in there? I mean the monitors were saying she flat lined."

"Her heart rate had dropped significantly due to the amount of blood lost she suffered and the stress of the situation. We gave her a shot of adrenaline and were able to get her heart pumping again. We also pumped a pint of blood into her system."

Tweety put her phone away and approached the conversation.

"So she's going to be alright?"

"She's going to be just fine, ma'am."

"Can we see her now?"

"Tomorrow. Tonight, she needs her rest." The doctor's pager went off. "I have to go. Congratulation, Mr. Bandz on your new baby." The doctor jogged over to another doctor then they bent the corner.

"That was Cadillac. He said the Feds told him they heard and recorded everything Aaron had confessed to at the apartments. With that, they got all the evidence they need to put the chief away for good."

"They can't put a warrant out for him. If he finds out they are on to him, then that recording we got won't mean shit to him. We'll have nothing to barter to get Lil Boss back."

"Princess, relax, Cadillac already thought of all that. The Feds agreed to let us do the exchange with Aaron first before they come after him."

"Ma, you and the girls stay here with Queenie and the baby."

"I'm not staying here, Boss. I'm coming with you to get my son." The look in her eyes told him she wasn't backing down or going to take no for an answer.

"Then, what are you waiting on? Let's go get our son." Boss could only hope the Feds kept their word. If not, there no way the Phantom was going to let Lil Boss or any of them live. If life's truly a gamble then Boss had everything the line and the pot is bigger than it has ever been for him. He could only hope he walks away a winner.

Chapter 28

Princess turned into the parking lot of 7 Mile Fair next to Hannah's BMW truck that Rome and Cadillac was riding in. Rome rolled down his window, Boss did the same. "What's the word, Boss?"

"I just texted him letting him know we're here." Overwhelmed with stress, Boss rubbed his face and caught a glimpse of himself in the sideview mirror. Bags under his eyes showed he hadn't had a good night's rest in over two days. Though rest was the farthest thing from his mind. He could only think about getting Lil Boss back so everything can be over with.

He got out the car with everyone else. His phone vibrated in his hand. It was a text from the Phantom. "He said once inside the gate we'll find one of his men selling live roosters near a van. He will lead us to the Phantom." They walked inside the swamp meet. Rome immediately took note of all the exits. Boss shared the same cautious mannerism.

"He arranged the switch at a public place and all. But I can't help but feel he has some type of underhanded trick up his sleeve."

"Boss, I believe we all would be fools to believe this exchange is going to go smooth. We're on our own too."

"The Feds aren't keeping close by?"

"They don't want to raise any suspicion. They want us to give the chief the phone with the recording and they're going to track him down using that." They past a crew setting up a vendor stand for the sale of car audio and subwoofers. They came upon the van with the chicken vendor.

"You gentlemen there!" Villa pointed at Boss and them. "You seem like the type of gentlemen that can appreciate a champion fighting rooster. I got just the one for you. Follow me!" Villa slicked his hair to the back as he led them through a catacomb of vendors. Each and every vendor they passed were on their hustle pressuring them to buy from them. An Asian lady selling bundles of socks for five dollars wouldn't take no for an answer until Villa physically pushed her aside. A mixture of popcorn, corn, spices, animal bedding and many other smells dominated the air inside.

Their journey through the maze of vendors ended at a door in the back of the building. Villa opened it with a key. The noise from outside became muffled once the door closed. The room looked like a shipping and receiving dock. Boxes were piled up in rows on pallets. Villa whistled the theme song to the Andy Griffin show as he continued to lead them further to the back of the room.

The chief stood in the back near the large garage doors. "You got that recording?"

"Yeah I got it." When they got close enough, three men came from behind the rows of boxes surrounding them with AR-15's in hand. "I thought we had a deal? Where's my son?" The chief gestured to Villa to open a door across the room.

"We do. This is just precaution. Our last meeting ended so messy."

"That was all on your account." Rome, pointed out.

The chief shrugged his shoulders with a smug look. "I see Boss brought his bitch. Where's that sexy lil Tweety bird of yours at, Cadillac?"

"Why, you trying to buy a taste?"

"That's funny. I bet you didn't know that on them lonely nights when you were gone, it was me keeping her bed warm."

Cadillac took a step closer and the men that surrounded them took aim at him. The chief waved his hand making them stand down.

"I bet you didn't know while you was stroking my woman, I was stroking your pockets." The chief gave him a look yeah right.

"Go back in time with me on this one playa. I want you to see the full picture. She called you every Friday night to come lay with her, right?" The chief folded his arms and kept listening. "Every Friday, at around a quarter to midnight, like clockwork, you would make rounds picking up money you got from shaking down pimps, whores and petty hustlers. You wouldn't count the money until you got home. But before you get home you would always get a call from Tweety to come over. You think I hadn't realize how infatuated you were with her? While you were living out your fantasy with her, I was in your car taking you for the price of that pussy and some. Shit, this nigga was paying more than her VIP tricks." Cadillac shared a laugh with Rome and the others. The chief turned red with embarrassment. The subject changed when in walked a man cradling Lil Boss with one arm.

"I'm sure you've met my protégé." Boss stared the man down. Princess tried to run to get Lil Boss but Boss held his arm out and stopped her.

"Indeed."

"You don't seem stunned to see me, Boss."

"You think I didn't know by now, Polo, that you been working for the Phantom? I'm a pimp, it's my job to stay ten steps ahead of hoes." Polo glanced at Princess knowing she put him up on game.

"You calling me a hoe? Bitch ass nigga I wear the crown in this pimp game. Recognize my royalty and show some respect."

The chief intervened cutting their argument short. "Gentlemen, gentlemen, let's get down to what we can here for. The recording please." He held out his hand to Cadillac. Cadillac pressed play and gave him the phone. The chief listened to it a few seconds then shut it off. "Give them kid and let's split."

Princess rushed over to get Lil Boss but Polo snatched him back. He took out his gun pointing it at Boss.

"I don't think so."

"What the hell you mean you don't think so? I don't have time for the testosterone dispute between you and Boss. Give them the kid and let's go!"

"Nah, see back at the apartments earlier when y'all slipped out the back I had my lil mans planted on the scene to keep an eye on what was going on. Lil bruh told me yo' boys Cadillac and Rome was chopping it up with the Feds. Word is they already have a copy of that recording. They coming for you."

"What?" The chief was walking in circle contemplating his next move. Panic was setting in. "Shit, we got to get out of here before they come for us!" The next thing he knew, three shots whispered off. The three men with the AR-15 laid on the ground in a pool of blood. The chief turned around and was face to face with the barrel of Villa's gun. "What the fuck's going on?"

"Welcome to your retirement party, chief."

"It's been a change of plans, chief. The Feds after you, not me. There's no use in destroying a perfectly good operation because it's founder fucked up. Consider me taking over things an honor to you." Polo held out his hand Villa handed him the gun.

"You shysty lil mothafucka."

PEWWW! Polo caught the chief right between the eyes. The chief's eyes rolled into the back of his head. Soon as he hit the ground with a heavy thud, Rome and Cadillac pulled out their heat. Boss pushed Princess out of the way and took out his. Polo put his gun to Lil Boss's head.

"Whoa! This ain't fair at all. This what's going to happen. Everyone but Boss, Princess and myself is going to leave the room."

"Like hell we will." Cadillac protested.

Polo pressed the barrel harder against the side of Lil Boss's head. "I will blow this lil nigga's thoughts across the room if my wishes ain't respected in the next ten seconds!"

"Get the hell out of here!" Princess cried, afraid of what Polo threatened to do to her son. Cadillac and Rome looked to Boss. Boss nodded to them. They left the room reluctantly behind Villa.

"Alright, they gone. What do you want?"

"Damn, can't we talk for a minute? We were best friends. Like brothers. That was until you played me shysty by stealing my bitch."

"I didn't steal from you, Polo. Listen, we can talk about whatever you want to talk about just take the gun away from his head."

"Nah, it's just fine where it's at. Tell me how long, Princess? How long you and my best friend been plotting behind my back to get together?" Princess could only shake her head with tears in her eyes. "Tell Me!"

"Calm down, Polo."

"Don't tell me to be calm. In fact, Boss, don't tell me shit but the truth to my questions. You know what, I got a game we can play to get the truth out." Polo laid Lil Boss on a stack of boxes and laid the gun down next to him. Then, he reached in the small of his back and pulled out a six shot .22. He shook out all but one bullet. He spun the cylinder then slapped it close.

"What are you doing, Polo?"

"Like I said, we going to play a little game. Y'all lie so good I can't tell when y'all telling the truth or telling a tale. So we going to let fate play the lie detector. Every time I ask the two of you a question and you answer I pull the trigger on this gun I got to the kid's head. If you telling the truth, he lives if not then heaven gets a new addition."

"What if we don't answer your questions?" Princess asked.

"I'll squeeze the trigger twice. First question has already been asked."

"I don't want to play this game."

"That's an unanswered question. You know what that means." He cocked back the hammer.

"Nooo!" Princess and Boss both yelled. Though it didn't stop Polo from squeezing the trigger…

Click! Click!

The gun landed on two empty chambers. He put another bullet in, spent the cylinder again and slapped it back close.

"Next question is for you, Boss. You never wanted me to be in the pimp game. You was afraid I was going to take that crown, wasn't you?

"You right, I didn't want you in the game."

"I knew it!"

"But not because I was afraid of you taking the crown. It was because I know what this game would do to you. I told you before, this game can't be played by just anybody. It takes a true pimp to do this shit."

"Then, I must be the best since I wear the crown."

"You could never be the best."

"Let's see if fate agree with that being true."

"Nooo!" Princess fell to the ground screaming.

"POLO STOP!"

He cocked back the slide on his gun and aimed it back at Polo's face. "Don't do this, bruh. I swear, you'll be making the greatest mistake in your life. You can't kill him, Polo." Flashes of Boss smiling in his face, then flashes of Boss and Princess making love to each other behind his back, flashed through his mind. Feelings of being played like a sucka by the two people he loved the most resurrected. He frowned, bit his lip, and pulled the trigger…

Click!

Boss found his breath when the hammer landed on another empty chamber. Princess was crying hysterically.

"Please stoppp! I'll do whatever you want. Just let my baby gooo!"

"Why should I stop, Princess? Huh? Why shouldn't I kill this living, breathing symbol of y'all betrayal?"

"Princess tell him," Boss told her without taking his eyes off Polo. Terrified, she turned to Boss and shook her head. "I can't." Her words were drowned by her sobbing but still heard.

"Princess, TELL HIM!"

"He's YOUR'S!"

"What the fuck you talking about?"

"Lil Boss is YOUR son, Polo." Princess broke down even harder.

"Stop lying! You two mothafuckas can quit trying to fuck with my head. The shit ain't working."

"We ain't fucking with yo head man. Princess, tell him."

She looked up at Boss with puppy dog eyes.

"Tell him."

Princess stood up, folding her arms across her chest. "After you done what you did to me, I didn't want anything more to do with you. I told Boss to tell you that I lost the baby, which I almost did thanks to you." Her eyes drifted over to Lil Boss who laid on the box gnawing on a teething ring. "But my lil man's a fighter." Her eyes fell back on Polo. Doubt was written all over his face. "Look at him Polo and tell me you don't see you in him. A blind man could see that's your son."

Polo couldn't believe what he was hearing. He looked down at Lil Boss. Lil Boss looked up at him with a bright smile. Polo felt like he'd been hit with a ton of bricks. Though Lil Boss took mostly after Princess, Polo still found his reflection in him. He smiled back at his son. He sat the gun down and picked him up. As he picked up Lil Boss, his other hand slipped out of sight and grabbed ahold to Villa's gun.

"So,, what was the plan here? To continue letting Boss play daddy to my son without letting me or my son knowing different?"

"I had no choice. Polo you ain't been right in the mind. What was I supposed to do ? Take a chance on you snapping out and hurting me and our son?"

"Polo, we did what we thought was best for Lil –
" *PEWWW! PEWWW!*

Polo hit Boss in the shoulder and the knee. The move caught Boss so far off guard his grip on the gun too relaxed to keep ahold to it when he hit the floor.

"OH MY GOD, BOSS!" Princess screamed. She ran to his side and cradled him in her arms.

"You was doing what you thought was best for MY son, Boss. Is that what you was going to tell me?" Princess was freaking out seeing the blood leaking out of Boss. "And you! You punk ass bitch. You say you didn't have a choice. Well, let me give you one. You can either let me walk out of here with your rights to my son signed over me or I'm going to put a hollow tip straight through Boss's skull. Make a choice!"

"Don't you give him, Lil Boss." Boss told her while fighting back the pain in his knee and shoulder.

"Sorry pimp, but the choice is not yours. Make a choice Princess or I'll just do both." Princess eyes darted from Boss to her son. She let go of Boss and took Lil Boss out of Polo's arms. Polo smiled at her decision.

She starred down at her baby boy a moment. "Boss, please forgive me."

"There's nothing to forgive." Boss was prepared to give his life for Lil Boss. He may not have been his biological son but to him he was still his son. Polo was ready to be the one to take Boss's existence off the earth.

Princess kissed Lil Boss's cheeks. "I will always love you baby." To both their surprise, she handed him over to Polo with tears showering down her face. "Take care of my son."

"What are you doing?" Boss dropped his head in failure.

"What's best."

"Boss, you must've fucked her brains out to make her do something as retarded as choose you over her own child. I would've enjoyed putting the final nail in your coffin, but this works out just as good. Even with the Phantom dead, I got enough juice in the police department to see to it that you keep you end of the deal. If the two of you want to continue living your happy lives, stay away from my son and make sure Cadillac and Rome don't mention me or Villa to the Feds. Understood?"

"Yes." Princess answered in a sobbing tone.

"And Boss, if you want to come back in the game you're more than welcome. But to do so, you'd have to kiss my feet and beg me in front of all the pimps and whores in the city." Polo laughed at him. "I'll send my attorney over in the morning for you to sign the papers. Later." Polo left out the back door with Lil Boss in his arms.

"Aggghhh!" Boss cringed as Princess helped him to his feet. "Why did you give him to him? You should've just let him kill me. Polo's going to destroy that boy's life." Princess felt truth in what Boss was saying. Though to her, she made the best decision. There was no other way to save the two people that meant the most to her. It was a decision she was prepared to live with.

Chapter 29

It's been six months since the drama at 7 Mile Fair. Things were starting to get back to normal for Boss and the family. Queenie and Boo Baby were out the hospital. Boss's leg was out of a cast and was walking with the assistance of a cane. Instead of being a unrecognized pimp in the game or begging Polo to let him back in, Boss opened Popping a night club in Madison Wisconsin near the UW college campus. He enrolled Gemini and Sapphire in school there and they brought the crowds to the club. He enrolled Isis in Marquette University to study to be a lawyer like she always wanted to be. Princess wanted nothing more than to tend to Boo Baby and help Boss care for Queenie. It took her mind away from the never ending heartache she had from not having Lil Boss around. Cadillac and Tweety were living life to the fullest traveling seeing the world and coming back to spoil their grandbaby. Rome had moved away to Nashville and opened up a escort service with star clients such as Tennessee Titans players. Everyone was putting the pieces of their life back together.

Rome closed the safe door shut pocketing an envelope full of cash he was about to deposit into the bank. He left out of his small office building and hopped into his AMG.

He was half mile down the road when his car began to act funny. He pulled to the side of the road and got out to analyze the car. His rear driver's side tire was on flat. He kneeled down for a closer examination. "What the hell." A piece of metal was stuck into it creating a slow leak.

A car pull over in front of his. It's car door open and footsteps trailed towards Rome. "You need a hand?" Rome was busy trying to get the piece of metal out of the tire and didn't bother to turn around.

"Unless you got a spare tire that'll fit or a flatbed truck I don't think so. I'ma call triple A and-"

Click! Clock! The man pressed the barrel off the gun to the back of his head.

"Triple A can't help you out of this one my nigga." Rome saw the man's reflection in his rims. He had forgotten one piece of unfinished business and it was going to cost him his life.

"Listen, I got your bread."

"Too late, times up."

"WAIT!" Parnell let off eleven shots into Rome. Then, stripped him of all his money and jewelry leaving him dead on the side of the road.

To Be Continued...

Lock Down Publications and Ca$h Presents
Assisted Publishing Packages

BASIC PACKAGE $499 Editing Cover Design Formatting	**UPGRADED PACKAGE** $800 Typing Editing Cover Design Formatting
ADVANCE PACKAGE $1,200 Typing Editing Cover Design Formatting Copyright registration Proofreading Upload book to Amazon	**LDP SUPREME PACKAGE** $1,500 Typing Editing Cover Design Formatting Copyright registration Proofreading Set up Amazon account Upload book to Amazon Advertise on LDP, Amazon and Facebook Page

***Other services available upon request.
Additional charges may apply

Lock Down Publications
P.O. Box 944
Stockbridge, GA 30281-9998
Phone: 470 303-9761

Submission Guideline

Submit the first three chapters of your completed manuscript to ldpsubmissions@gmail.com. In the subject line add **Your Book's Title**. The manuscript must be in a Word Doc file and sent as an attachment. Document should be in Times New Roman, double spaced, and in size 12 font. Also, provide your synopsis and full contact information. If sending multiple submissions, they must each be in a separate email.

Have a story but no way to send it electronically? You can still submit to LDP/Ca$h Presents. Send in the first three chapters, written or typed, of your completed manuscript to:

LDP: Submissions Dept
P.O. Box 944
Stockbridge, GA 30281-9998

DO NOT send original manuscript. Must be a duplicate. Provide your synopsis and a cover letter containing your full contact information.

Thanks for considering LDP and Ca$h Presents.

NEW RELEASES

BLOODLINE OF A SAVAGE 1&2
THESE VICIOUS STREETS
RELENTLESS GOON
RELENTLESS GOON 2
BY PRINCE A. TAUHID

THE BUTTERFLY MAFIA 1-3
BY FUMIYA PAYNE

A THUG'S STREET PRINCESS 1&2
BY MEESHA

CITY OF SMOKE 2
BY MOLOTTI

STEPPERS 1,2&3
BY KING RIO

THE LANE 1&2
BY KEN-KEN SPENCE

THUG OF SPADES 1&2
LOVE IN THE TRENCHES 2
BY COREY ROBINSON

TIL DEATH 3
BY ARYANNA

THE BIRTH OF A GANGSTER 4
BY DELMONT PLAYER

BLOOD AND GAMES 2 | KING DREAM

PRODUCT OF THE STREETS 1&2
BY DEMOND "MONEY" ANDERSON

NO TIME FOR ERROR
BY KEESE

MONEY HUNGRY DEMONS
BY TRANAY ADAMS

Coming Soon from Lock Down Publications/Ca$h Presents

IF YOU CROSS ME ONCE 6
ANGEL V
By Anthony Fields

IMMA DIE BOUT MINE 4&5
By Aryanna

A THUGS STREET PRINCESS 3
By Meesha

PRODUCT OF THE STREETS 3
By Demond Money Anderson

CORNER BOYS
By Corey Robinson

SON OF A DOPE FIEND 4
By Renta

THE MURDER QUEENS 6&7
By Michael Gallon

CITY OF SMOKE 3
By Molotti

BETRAYAL OF A G
By Ray Vinci

CONFESSIONS OF A DOPE BOY
By Nicholas Lock

THA TAKEOVER
By Keith Chandler

Available Now

RESTRAINING ORDER 1 & 2
By **CA$H & Coffee**

LOVE KNOWS NO BOUNDARIES 1-3
By **Coffee**

RAISED AS A GOON I, II, III & IV
BRED BY THE SLUMS I, II, III
BLAST FOR ME I & II
ROTTEN TO THE CORE I II III
A BRONX TALE I, II, III
DUFFLE BAG CARTEL I II III IV V VI
HEARTLESS GOON I II III IV V
A SAVAGE DOPEBOY I II
DRUG LORDS I II III
CUTTHROAT MAFIA I II
KING OF THE TRENCHES
By **Ghost**

LAY IT DOWN I & II
LAST OF A DYING BREED I II
BLOOD STAINS OF A SHOTTA I & II III
By **Jamaica**

LOYAL TO THE GAME I II III
LIFE OF SIN I, II III
By **TJ & Jelissa**

IF LOVING HIM IS WRONG…I & II
LOVE ME EVEN WHEN IT HURTS I II III
By **Jelissa**

BLOODY COMMAS I & II
SKI MASK CARTEL I, II & III
KING OF NEW YORK I II, III IV V
RISE TO POWER I II III
COKE KINGS I II III IV V
BORN HEARTLESS I II III IV
KING OF THE TRAP I II
By **T.J. Edwards**

WHEN THE STREETS CLAP BACK I & II III
THE HEART OF A SAVAGE I II III IV
MONEY MAFIA I II
LOYAL TO THE SOIL I II III
By **Jibril Williams**

A DISTINGUISHED THUG STOLE MY HEART I II &
III
LOVE SHOULDN'T HURT I II III IV
RENEGADE BOYS 1-4
PAID IN KARMA 1-3
SAVAGE STORMS 1-3
AN UNFORESEEN LOVE 1-3
BABY, I'M WINTERTIME COLD 1-3
A THUG'S STREET PRINCESS 1&2
By **Meesha**

A GANGSTER'S CODE 1-3
A GANGSTER'S SYN 1-3
THE SAVAGE LIFE 1-3
CHAINED TO THE STREETS 1-3
BLOOD ON THE MONEY 1-3
A GANGSTA'S PAIN 1-3
BEAUTIFUL LIES AND UGLY TRUTHS
CHURCH IN THESE STREETS
By **J-Blunt**

PUSH IT TO THE LIMIT
By **Bre' Hayes**

BLOOD OF A BOSS 1-5
SHADOWS OF THE GAME
TRAP BASTARD
By **Askari**

THE STREETS BLEED MURDER 1-3
THE HEART OF A GANGSTA 1-3
By **Jerry Jackson**

CUM FOR ME 1-8
An LDP Erotica Collaboration

BRIDE OF A HUSTLA 1-3
THE FETTI GIRLS 1-3
CORRUPTED BY A GANGSTA 1-4
BLINDED BY HIS LOVE
THE PRICE YOU PAY FOR LOVE 1-3
DOPE GIRL MAGIC 1-3
By **Destiny Skai**

WHEN A GOOD GIRL GOES BAD
By **Adrienne**

A KINGPIN'S AMBITION
A KINGPIN'S AMBITION II
I MURDER FOR THE DOUGH
By **Ambitious**

THE COST OF LOYALTY 1-3
By **Kweli**

A GANGSTER'S REVENGE 1-4
THE BOSS MAN'S DAUGHTERS 1-5
A SAVAGE LOVE 1&2
BAE BELONGS TO ME 1&2
A HUSTLER'S DECEIT 1-3
WHAT BAD BITCHES DO 1-3
SOUL OF A MONSTER 1-3
KILL ZONE
A DOPE BOY'S QUEEN 1-3
TIL DEATH 1-3
IMMA DIE BOUT MINE 1-3
By **Aryanna**

TRUE SAVAGE 1-7
DOPE BOY MAGIC 1-3
MIDNIGHT CARTEL 1-3
CITY OF KINGZ 1&2
NIGHTMARE ON SILENT AVE
THE PLUG OF LIL MEXICO 1&2
CLASSIC CITY
By **Chris Green**

A DOPEBOY'S PRAYER
By **Eddie "Wolf" Lee**

THE KING CARTEL 1-3
By **Frank Gresham**

THESE NIGGAS AIN'T LOYAL 1-3
By **Nikki Tee**

GANGSTA SHYT 1-3
By **CATO**

THE ULTIMATE BETRAYAL
By **Phoenix**

BOSS'N UP 1-3
By **Royal Nicole**

I LOVE YOU TO DEATH
By **Destiny J**

I RIDE FOR MY HITTA
I STILL RIDE FOR MY HITTA
By **Misty Holt**

LOVE & CHASIN' PAPER
By **Qay Crockett**

TO DIE IN VAIN
SINS OF A HUSTLA
By **ASAD**

BROOKLYN HUSTLAZ
By **Boogsy Morina**

BROOKLYN ON LOCK 1 & 2
By **Sonovia**

GANGSTA CITY
By **Teddy Duke**

A DRUG KING AND HIS DIAMOND 1-3
A DOPEMAN'S RICHES
HER MAN, MINE'S TOO 1&2
CASH MONEY HO'S
THE WIFEY I USED TO BE 1&2
PRETTY GIRLS DO NASTY THINGS
By **Nicole Goosby**

LIPSTICK KILLAH 1-3
CRIME OF PASSION 1-3
FRIEND OR FOE 1-3
By **Mimi**

TRAPHOUSE KING 1-3
KINGPIN KILLAZ 1-3
STREET KINGS 1&2
PAID IN BLOOD 1&2
CARTEL KILLAZ 1-3
DOPE GODS 1&2
By **Hood Rich**

STEADY MOBBN' 1-3
THE STREETS STAINED MY SOUL 1-3
By **Marcellus Allen**

WHO SHOT YA 1-3
SON OF A DOPE FIEND 1-3
HEAVEN GOT A GHETTO 1&2
SKI MASK MONEY 1&2
By **Renta**

GORILLAZ IN THE BAY 1-4
TEARS OF A GANGSTA 1/&2
3X KRAZY 1&2
STRAIGHT BEAST MODE 1&2
By **DE'KARI**

TRIGGADALE 1-3
MURDA WAS THE CASE 1-3
By **Elijah R. Freeman**

THE STREETS ARE CALLING
By **Duquie Wilson**

SLAUGHTER GANG 1-3
RUTHLESS HEART 1-3
By **Willie Slaughter**

GOD BLESS THE TRAPPERS 1-3
THESE SCANDALOUS STREETS 1-3
FEAR MY GANGSTA 1-5
THESE STREETS DON'T LOVE NOBODY 1-2
BURY ME A G 1-5
A GANGSTA'S EMPIRE 1-4
THE DOPEMAN'S BODYGAURD 1&2
THE REALEST KILLAZ 1-3
THE LAST OF THE OGS 1-3
By **Tranay Adams**

MARRIED TO A BOSS 1-3
By **Destiny Skai & Chris Green**

KINGZ OF THE GAME 1-7
CRIME BOSS 1-3
By **Playa Ray**

FUK SHYT
By **Blakk Diamond**

DON'T F#CK WITH MY HEART 1&2
By **Linnea**

ADDICTED TO THE DRAMA 1-3
IN THE ARM OF HIS BOSS
By **Jamila**

LOYALTY AIN'T PROMISED 1&2
By **Keith Williams**

YAYO 1-4
A SHOOTER'S AMBITION 1&2
BRED IN THE GAME
By **S. Allen**

TRAP GOD 1-3
RICH $AVAGE 1-3
MONEY IN THE GRAVE 1-3
CARTEL MONEY
By **Martell Troublesome Bolden**

FOREVER GANGSTA 1&2
GLOCKS ON SATIN SHEETS 1&2
By **Adrian Dulan**

TOE TAGZ 1-4
LEVELS TO THIS SHYT 1&2
IT'S JUST ME AND YOU
By **Ah'Million**

KINGPIN DREAMS 1-3
RAN OFF ON DA PLUG
By **Paper Boi Rari**

CONFESSIONS OF A GANGSTA 1-4
CONFESSIONS OF A JACKBOY 1-3
CONFESSIONS OF A HITMAN
By **Nicholas Lock**

I'M NOTHING WITHOUT HIS LOVE
SINS OF A THUG
TO THE THUG I LOVED BEFORE
A GANGSTA SAVED XMAS
IN A HUSTLER I TRUST
By **Monet Dragun**

QUIET MONEY 1-3
THUG LIFE 1-3
EXTENDED CLIP 1&2
A GANGSTA'S PARADISE
By **Trai'Quan**

CAUGHT UP IN THE LIFE 1-3
THE STREETS NEVER LET GO 1-3
By **Robert Baptiste**

NEW TO THE GAME 1-3
MONEY, MURDER & MEMORIES 1-3
By **Malik D. Rice**

CREAM 2-3
THE STREETS WILL TALK
By **Yolanda Moore**

LIFE OF A SAVAGE 1-4
A GANGSTA'S QUR'AN 1-4
MURDA SEASON 1-3
GANGLAND CARTEL 1-3
CHI'RAQ GANGSTAS 1-4
KILLERS ON ELM STREET 1-3
JACK BOYZ N DA BRONX 1-3
A DOPEBOY'S DREAM 1-3
JACK BOYS VS DOPE BOYS 1-3
COKE GIRLZ
COKE BOYS
SOSA GANG 1&2
BRONX SAVAGES
BODYMORE KINGPINS
BLOOD OF A GOON
By **Romell Tukes**

BLOOD AND GAMES 2 | KING DREAM

THE STREETS MADE ME 1-3
By **Larry D. Wright**

CONCRETE KILLA 1-3
VICIOUS LOYALTY 1-3
By **Kingpen**

THE ULTIMATE SACRIFICE 1-6
KHADIFI
IF YOU CROSS ME ONCE 1-3
ANGEL 1-4
IN THE BLINK OF AN EYE
By **Anthony Fields**

THE LIFE OF A HOOD STAR
By **Ca$h & Rashia Wilson**

THE STREETS WILL NEVER CLOSE 1-3
By **K'ajji**

NIGHTMARES OF A HUSTLA 1-3
By **King Dream**

HARD AND RUTHLESS 1&2
MOB TOWN 251
THE BILLIONAIRE BENTLEYS 1-3
REAL G'S MOVE IN SILENCE
By **Von Diesel**

GHOST MOB
By **Stilloan Robinson**

MOB TIES 1-6
SOUL OF A HUSTLER, HEART OF A KILLER 1-3
GORILLAZ IN THE TRENCHES
By **SayNoMore**

BODYMORE MURDERLAND 1-3
THE BIRTH OF A GANGSTER 1-4
By **Delmont Player**

FOR THE LOVE OF A BOSS 1&2
By **C. D. Blue**

KILLA KOUNTY 1-5
By **Khufu**

MOBBED UP 1-4
THE BRICK MAN 1-5
THE COCAINE PRINCESS 1-10
STEPPERS 1-3
SUPER GREMLIN 1-4
By **King Rio**

MONEY GAME 1&2
By **Smoove Dolla**

A GANGSTA'S KARMA 1-4
By **FLAME**

KING OF THE TRENCHES 1-3
By **GHOST & TRANAY ADAMS**

QUEEN OF THE ZOO 1&2
By **Black Migo**

GRIMEY WAYS 1-3
By **Ray Vinci**

XMAS WITH AN ATL SHOOTER
By **Ca$h & Destiny Skai**

BLOOD AND GAMES 2 | KING DREAM

KING KILLA 1&2
By **Vincent "Vitto" Holloway**

BETRAYAL OF A THUG 1&2
By **Fre$h**

THE MURDER QUEENS 1-5
By **Michael Gallon**

FOR THE LOVE OF BLOOD 1-4
By **Jamel Mitchell**

HOOD CONSIGLIERE 1&2
NO TIME FOR ERROR
By **Keese**

PROTÉGÉ OF A LEGEND 1&2
LOVE IN THE TRENCHES 1&2
By **Corey Robinson**

BORN IN THE GRAVE 1-3
CRIME PAYS
By **Self Made Tay**

MOAN IN MY MOUTH
By **XTASY**

TORN BETWEEN A GANGSTER AND A GENTLEMAN
By **J-BLUNT & Miss Kim**

LOYALTY IS EVERYTHING 1-3
CITY OF SMOKE 1&2
By **Molotti**

HERE TODAY GONE TOMORROW 1&2
By **Fly Rock**

WOMEN LIE MEN LIE 1-4
FIFTY SHADES OF SNOW 1-3
STACK BEFORE YOU SPLURGE
GIRLS FALL LIKE DOMINOES
NAÏVE TO THE STREETS
By **ROY MILLIGAN**

PILLOW PRINCESS
By **S. Hawkins**

THE BUTTERFLY MAFIA 1-3
SALUTE MY SAVAGERY 1&2
By **Fumiya Payne**

THE LANE 1&2
By Ken-Ken Spence

THE PUSSY TRAP 1-5
By **Nene Capri**

DIRTY DNA
By **Blaque**

SANCTIFIED AND HORNY
by **XTASY**

BOOKS BY LDP'S CEO, CA$H

TRUST IN NO MAN
TRUST IN NO MAN 2
TRUST IN NO MAN 3
BONDED BY BLOOD
SHORTY GOT A THUG
THUGS CRY
THUGS CRY 2
THUGS CRY 3
TRUST NO BITCH
TRUST NO BITCH 2
TRUST NO BITCH 3
TIL MY CASKET DROPS
RESTRAINING ORDER
RESTRAINING ORDER 2
IN LOVE WITH A CONVICT
LIFE OF A HOOD STAR
XMAS WITH AN ATL SHOOTER

www.ingramcontent.com/pod-product-compliance
Lightning Source LLC
Chambersburg PA
CBHW060641260626
47161CB00008B/2942